The
ARABIAN
NIGHTS

In the name
of the most high,
the merciful, the compassionate
Creator of the Universe
in whom I trust,
may the tales of olden time
be lessons for
the people of
our day.

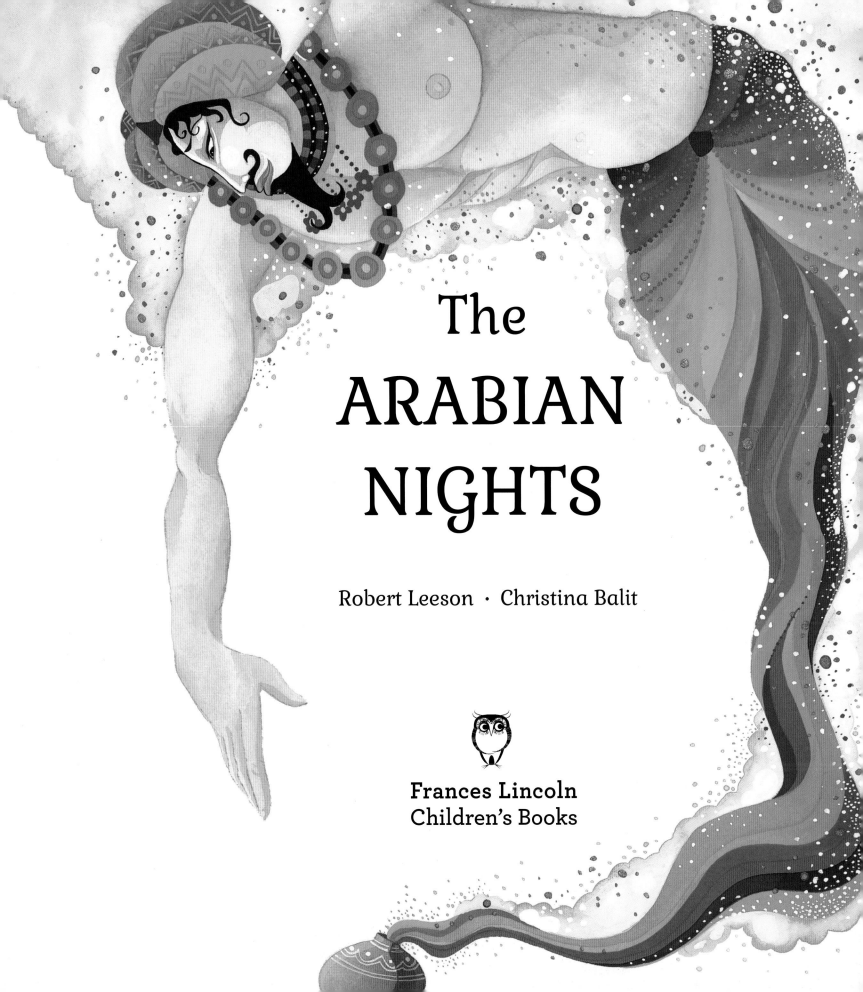

The
ARABIAN
NIGHTS

Robert Leeson · Christina Balit

Frances Lincoln
Children's Books

For Christine — R.L.

For a special friend, Tessa — C.B.

.·.
·.·

Text copyright © Robert Leeson 2001
Illustrations copyright © Christina Balit 2001

First published as *My Sister, Shahrazad* in Great Britain in 2001
by Frances Lincoln Children's Books
This edition first published in Great Britain and the USA in 2015
by Frances Lincoln Children's Books,
74–77 White Lion Street, London N1 9PF
www.franceslincoln.com

British Library Cataloguing in Publication Data available on request

ISBN 978-1-84780-715-1

Printed in China

1 3 5 7 9 8 6 4 2

Contents

Prologue

King Shahrayar *ruled the empires of the East and his brother Shahzaman the far kingdom of Samarkand. They were mighty in war and just in peace. All who dwelt in their shadow prospered.*

My sister Shahrazad and I, Dunyazad, lived in the palace of our father, the king's wazir, or chief minister. We passed our days in pleasant pastimes, without a care in the world.

Then one day, when Shahrazad was sixteen and I, Dunyazad, was thirteen, a calamity struck the kingdom. King Shahrayar's wife betrayed him with a slave from the royal household. And as Fate would have it, the same misfortune befell the king's brother. But that was only the beginning. What followed cast a dark cloud over the realm.

For the king had his wife put to death. Then, declaring that no woman was to be trusted, he took a young virgin from the highest family to his bedchamber, and after one night he summoned his wazir and commanded him: "Take her to the executioner."

Horrified, but not daring to disobey, our father led the innocent girl to her death. The next night, another girl was taken to the king's bed and again, with the dawn, her head fell to the executioner's blade. So the nightmare went on: princesses, merchants' daughters, young women of the common people alike, were taken and slaughtered.

People whispered, "The king is mad." Those with great wealth took their daughters and fled to far countries. Those who could not escape waited in fear. But none dared speak aloud. The kingdom groaned while its daughters died.

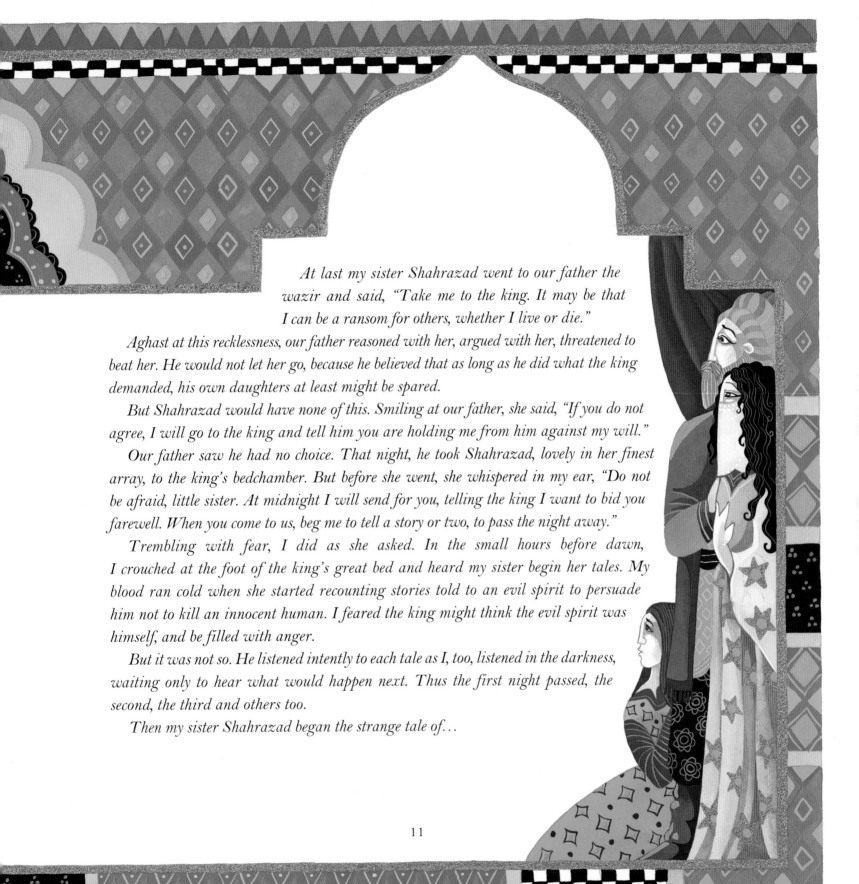

At last my sister Shahrazad went to our father the wazir and said, "Take me to the king. It may be that I can be a ransom for others, whether I live or die."

Aghast at this recklessness, our father reasoned with her, argued with her, threatened to beat her. He would not let her go, because he believed that as long as he did what the king demanded, his own daughters at least might be spared.

But Shahrazad would have none of this. Smiling at our father, she said, "If you do not agree, I will go to the king and tell him you are holding me from him against my will."

Our father saw he had no choice. That night, he took Shahrazad, lovely in her finest array, to the king's bedchamber. But before she went, she whispered in my ear, "Do not be afraid, little sister. At midnight I will send for you, telling the king I want to bid you farewell. When you come to us, beg me to tell a story or two, to pass the night away."

Trembling with fear, I did as she asked. In the small hours before dawn, I crouched at the foot of the king's great bed and heard my sister begin her tales. My blood ran cold when she started recounting stories told to an evil spirit to persuade him not to kill an innocent human. I feared the king might think the evil spirit was himself, and be filled with anger.

But it was not so. He listened intently to each tale as I, too, listened in the darkness, waiting only to hear what would happen next. Thus the first night passed, the second, the third and others too.

Then my sister Shahrazad began the strange tale of…

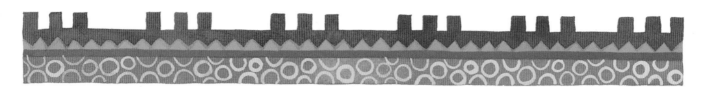

The Fisherman and the Jinni

Know, O King, that there was once a poor fisherman who had a wife and three daughters. They all lived on what he could harvest from the sea. Every morning, while the moon still hung in the sky, he rose and went down to the shore. He cast his nets into the water four times, waiting to see what his catch might be.

On this day, of all days, he waded into the water to his knees and spun his nets through the air until they sank beneath the waves. When he tugged on the lines, how heavy they felt! Overjoyed at the thought of a rich haul of fish, he rushed forward until he was up to his waist in sea water, and dragged his nets to land.

Imagine how his heart sank when he saw that a dead donkey was trapped in the meshes! Yet he did not curse, but only raised his eyes to heaven, said a silent prayer, and cast again. Once more his hopes were dashed, for he had caught nothing but an old cooking pot.

A third time his nets vanished into the depths. This time they rose loaded with stones and rubbish.

Raising his head in despair, he prayed once more, for this was his last chance. He never tried more than four times, for fear of bad fortune. This time, so heavy was the burden of his nets, he was forced to plunge beneath the waves. It took all his strength to bring his catch to shore.

There in the nets lay a great jar made of copper, green with age. Its mouth was sealed and the seal inscribed with ancient writing which he could not read.

"Copper!" he cried. "If I can carry this to market and sell it, we shall live well for a month. But first I must empty out what is inside." So saying, he cut open the seal.

At once a thick cloud of smoke rushed from the neck of the jar and spread out until it filled the skies. There it formed into a monstrous jinni, or spirit, high as a mountain, with legs as tall as ships' masts, a mouth like a cavern, teeth like tombstones and eyes like blazing lamps.

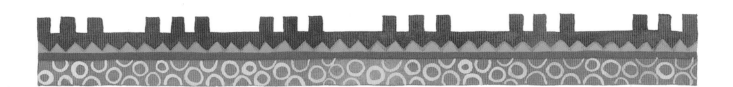

As the fisherman cowered on the sand, the monster cried in a voice like thunder, "O great Solomon, forgive me! I will never disobey you again."

Forgetting his fear, the astonished fisherman cried out, "Why do you call on Solomon? He has been dead these two thousand years."

At these words, the jinni laughed a gigantic laugh and cried, "I am free!" Then he bent down his hideous face and said, "Mortal, it is you who have released me. I shall grant you a wish." But, before the fisherman could find his voice, his insides turned to water, for the jinni went on, "Tell me how you wish to die."

"To d-die?" stammered the fisherman. "Why should you take my life when I have just freed you, O unjust spirit?"

"O insect," roared the jinni. "Why ask foolish questions? I could kill you now, but as a reward I grant you this wish: choose how you would die."

Out of his wits with terror, the fisherman remained silent. So the jinni spoke again:

"Know, O worm, that I was one of the jinni that rebelled against the great Lord Solomon. When we were defeated, he punished me by making this copper jar my prison. As the ages passed, I longed for deliverance. I promised that he who set me free would be rich for life. But no deliverer came, though countless years went by.

"Then I promised that whoever freed me should be rewarded with all the treasures of the earth. A hundred, two hundred, three hundred years went by, but still no one came. Then I swore that my liberator should be king and I would serve him day and night. But my dungeon door stayed shut.

"At last my mood darkened with impatience. I grew angry in my dank cell. And I swore a great oath: that whoever opened this door should die, in revenge for my ordeal.

"So now," said the jinni, "choose how I shall kill you."

Desperate to gain a little more time to live, the fisherman began to tell the jinni stories of mercy and of treachery. He told how a king, led astray by bad advice, condemned to death the doctor who had cured him of a terrible illness. But even as the doctor died, he succeeded in poisoning the king. "Injustice is surely punished by death," cried the fisherman.

But the jinni only laughed until the sky shook.

"Don't waste my time, O miserable one. Choose the manner of your death, and choose quickly."

Staring death in the face, the fisherman said to himself, "The spirits are all-powerful. Yet we mortals still have our wits."

So he spoke out boldly: "O, most potent lord, if I ask you one last question before you end my unworthy life, will you answer it truly?"

"What, more questions?" bellowed the giant. "Well – one question, then."

"Tell me, O mighty one," said the fisherman humbly, "if your head touches the clouds, and your breadth is like a mountain, how did you spend two thousand years in that small jar? It is not to be believed."

The jinni ground his teeth like clashing rocks. "I tell you, I did – may you die slowly and in torment."

"Then how did you get inside, O potent one?"

"Like this!"

And with a roar of impatience like ten thousand lions, the jinni turned himself into a cloud of smoke, which dwindled until it vanished inside the copper jar.

With trembling fingers, the fisherman took the seal with the name of the great Solomon inscribed on it and clapped it into the neck of the jar. From inside came a hollow howl of fury, as the jinni realised he had been tricked.

All at once his voice became soft and pleading.

"Most noble sir," he begged, "free me once more, and I will make you rich."

But the fisherman laughed harshly. "O enemy to truth and trust, you shall stay prisoner beneath these waves until the end of time. I shall warn all fishermen on this shore whose nets may drag you up again by chance, and they will cast you back."

"I beseech you," whimpered the jinni. "I am wicked, but you are a good man. Let us go by your rules, not mine. Forgive me, and you will have cause to be thankful."

The fisherman thought for a while, then said, "Do you swear by the name of One on High not to harm me?"

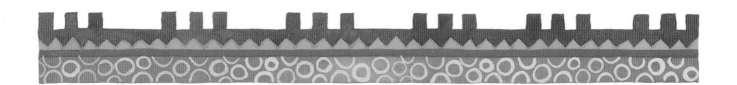

The jinni swallowed his pride. "I do, I do," he murmured.

At this, the fisherman knocked away the magic seal and, with the sound of a thousand rushing whirlwinds, the smoke poured out. Once more the jinni towered over the sea and shore. With a laugh of fiendish glee the monster kicked the jar into the sea. Then he turned a face full of malevolence upon the one who had freed him not once, but twice. The fisherman grovelled on the ground, wetting himself with terror.

"I call on you in the most Sacred Name," he begged. "Remember your oath!"

The jinni roared with laughter. "Fear not, worm, but follow me," he said. Still shaking, the fisherman followed.

They marched into the mountains and there, by the side of a deep dark lake, the jinni halted, saying, "Look!" The fisherman stared at the water, which swarmed with miraculous fish, white, red, blue and yellow.

The jinni spoke. "Cast your net," he said. "Take your catch to the sultan and he will reward you greatly. Only one warning: do not fish here more than once a day, or the fish will disappear. Now, cunning mortal, farewell!"

With that, the jinni stamped his foot and was swallowed up by the earth, leaving the fisherman astonished, but happy beyond belief.

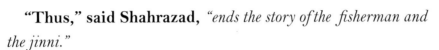

"Thus," said Shahrazad, *"ends the story of the fisherman and the jinni."*

"It was truly marvellous," said King Shahrayar.

"But not so marvellous as the story of the jester," answered my sister.

"Tell on," said the king, his eyes agleam.

But Shahrazad pointed to the window. "See, O Prince, it is dawn. Yet if my lord wishes, he shall hear that story when night comes again, if his servant is spared so long."

That morning I, Dunyazad, went to the lattice window from which women may look down unseen on the Hall of Judgement. There sat King Shahrayar in all his power and glory, rewarding or condemning those who came before him. And there at his side stood my father the wazir, his face lined with grief. Over his arm he bore a shroud for my sister Shahrazad. For he believed that today he must lead his daughter to the executioner.

My heart was sad that I could not relieve his pain, for I was sworn to secrecy. But my heart was glad because I knew my sister would not die that day.

And so, when the midnight hour was past, Shahrazad began...

The Story of the Jester

It is told, O King of Time, though only One Above knows all, that long ago in a distant city lived a tailor and his wife, and they were a merry couple.

Late one evening, to amuse themselves, they were wandering through the bustling market streets, watching folk buy and sell, while storytellers and musicians entertained the crowds.

Just as they were turning to go home for supper, they saw the strangest sight. A little hunchbacked jester, gaily dressed and drunk as a lord, was turning somersaults and telling jokes. So comical was he that the tailor's wife said, "Let's invite the jester home for supper."

No sooner said than done. The little man gladly joined them and enjoyed the food and drink they offered him. He sang so well for his supper that they were delighted.

Then a terrible thing happened. They urged their guest to eat the last fish left on the plate. He protested, "Thank you, thank you. I couldn't eat another crumb." But in foolish jest they stuffed the fish into the jester's mouth. He swallowed, choked, turned red, then a ghastly white and, falling down in front of them, lay still and stiff.

"Alas," cried the tailor. "We have killed him. I shall lose my head for this."

"Fool, you have lost it already," said his wife. "Now listen. Wrap the jester in this blanket. Pick him up, for he weighs no more than a boy, and follow me."

Trembling, the tailor obeyed his wife and they went out into the crowded street. People soon made way, when the tailor's wife called out, "A doctor! Where may we find a doctor? I fear our little boy may have the smallpox."

Thus they reached the home of the Jewish physician, where they gave his servant money to call her master down.

As soon as the servant had gone upstairs, the tailor's wife said, "Now, be quick. Put the jester on the stairs and let us be gone." This was done and all seemed well. But worse was to come.

In his haste to reach the sick person, the physician rushed downstairs in his

nightshirt. His foot struck the little man and hurled his body downstairs to the ground where it lay still.

"My life," cried the physician. "I, who should heal, have killed a stranger. What shall I do?"

His wife, who had got out of bed with him, kept a cool head. "Lift up the body, husband. Carry it to the roof and we will lower it into the back yard of our neighbour the steward. It is so tightly packed with bags of grain and jars of oil, no one will see the body until the morning."

This was done, and back they went to bed. But in the small hours the steward came home, and by the light of the risen moon he saw a shadow on the wall of his yard.

"At last!" he crowed, "The thief who has been looting my stores is caught in the act."

With these words he charged out, stick in hand, and gave the jester, whose body leant against the wall, a terrible blow. Without a word, the body rolled over and lay still as a stone.

"I am a lost man," the steward whispered in alarm. "I meant to punish, but I have killed. I will die for this." But not just yet, he thought.

Heaving the body over his shoulder, he stole down the alleys behind his house until he found a dark corner. There he left the little jester slumped against a wall, looking for all the world like a tired reveller. Then the steward stole silently back to his bed.

No sooner had he gone, than a Christian broker who had been celebrating with friends came by on his way home. Seeing the figure crouched in the shadows, he thought nervously, "That man is waiting to snatch my turban, just as those rascals did earlier this evening. Well, he's going to get a surprise."

With that, he sprang forward and gave the ambusher such a blow that he flew halfway across the narrow street and lay still.

Aghast, the broker muttered, "God help me, I've killed him!" and turned to flee.

Too late. He was seen by two market guards. Seizing the broker, they marched him off to the wali, or police chief, while a crowd of idlers followed them, carrying the jester's body and clamouring, "Justice! Justice!"

When the wali learnt that a Christian had murdered a Moslem, he ordered the body and

the accused to be taken to the city governor. The governor sent word to the sultan, and soon came back the dire command, "Let the guilty hang."

The dreadful news spread like wildfire. At first light, the executioner and his assistant erected a gallows in the main city square, where it seemed the whole population had gathered. "Justice! Justice!" they roared.

But no sooner was the noose around the broker's neck, than a voice called out from the crowd. It was the steward. The crowd fell silent as he spoke these trembling words: "Justice, my Lord Governor. Let not a Christian die for the crime a Moslem has committed."

Quickly he told how he had struck down the jester, believing him to be a thief. Amazed, the governor ordered the executioner to free the broker and hang the steward.

Hardly had the rope circled the newly-condemned man's neck, when there was another disturbance in the crowd. It was the physician, crying, "Justice, O Great One! Let not a Moslem die for the wrong a Jew has done."

All gaped in silence as the physician and the steward changed places on the scaffold. Grumbling at the extra trouble he was being put to, the executioner prepared once more to do his duty. But yet again he was thwarted, this time by the tailor, who rushed forward shouting out his guilt.

By now the executioner had had enough. How could a craftsman get on with his work? "Your Honour," he said to the governor, "there are a thousand people here. Suppose they are all tired of life?"

How the crowd roared! But this time, it was with laughter. The governor commanded, "Let anyone who desires to take the tailor's place step forward." Silence fell. "Very well," said the governor, and he gave the sign for the executioner to hang the tailor.

But yet again there was an interruption. On the palace balcony above the square appeared the sultan himself. Woken from his sleep, he had been told the strange story of the four murders of one victim. And he realised that the dead man was none other than his own jester, missing since the day before. His mood was stern.

"Never before have I heard so strange a story. The broker, the steward, the physician and

the tailor are all worthy men. But each in his own way is guilty of my servant's death. Now, hear me: unless any one of you can tell me a story more amazing than that of the jester, all of you must die."

A deeper silence fell over the city square as, one by one, the broker, the physician and the steward told a story. Each tale was stranger and more wonderful than the last; yet still the sultan, who prized his jester highly, was not satisfied.

"Speak now, tailor. Your life and that of these three men are in your hands. Tell a story to astonish me, or all of you will surely hang."

A thousand pairs of eyes fixed on the tailor as the crowd waited for his tale.

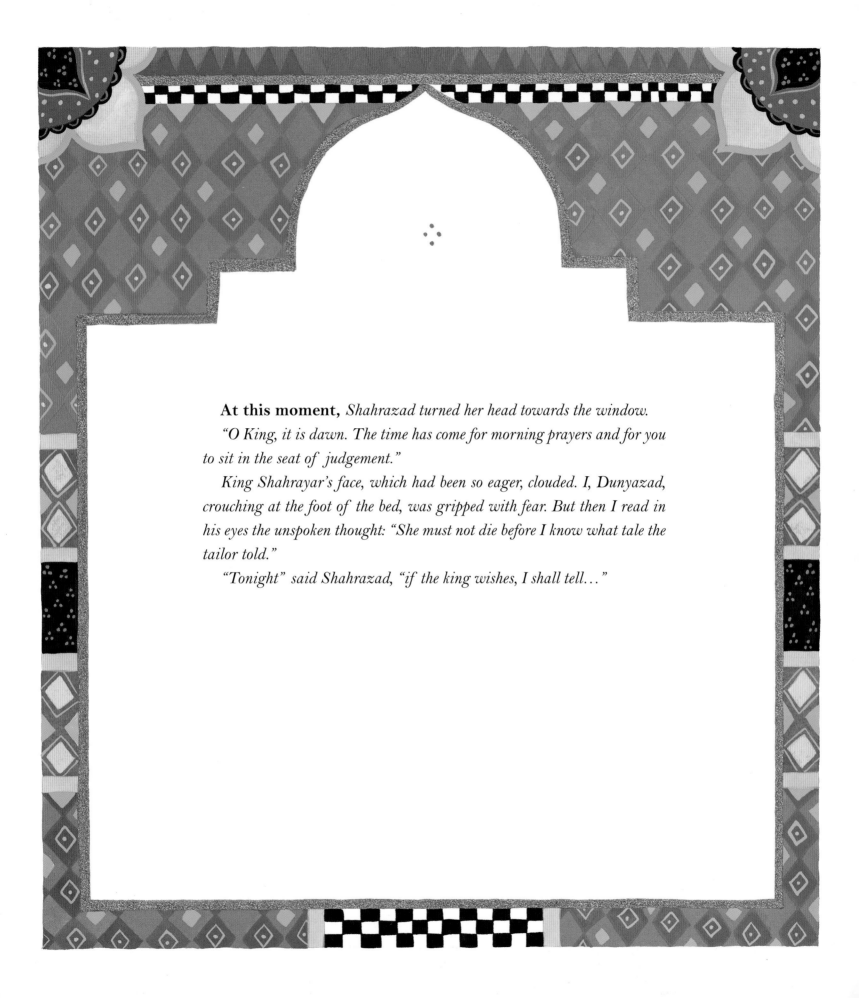

At this moment, *Shahrazad turned her head towards the window.*

"O King, it is dawn. The time has come for morning prayers and for you to sit in the seat of judgement."

King Shahrayar's face, which had been so eager, clouded. I, Dunyazad, crouching at the foot of the bed, was gripped with fear. But then I read in his eyes the unspoken thought: "She must not die before I know what tale the tailor told."

"Tonight" said Shahrazad, "if the king wishes, I shall tell…"

The Tailor's Story of The Lame Young Man and the Barber

"Yesterday, O Mighty One," said the tailor, "I sat with my companions, fellow craftsmen, and passed a pleasant hour. With us was a stranger, a young merchant from a far city, courteous, handsome, but lame in one leg.

Suddenly, he rose, crying, and said, 'I will not eat with that scoundrel.' He was pointing at an old man, a well-known barber of the town.

'He,' declared the young man, 'is the cause of my misfortune.'

We begged him to explain this astounding accusation and here, my lord, is his story:

'I was born in the splendid city of Baghdad, and since my father was one of its wealthiest merchants, life's gifts were showered upon me. Yet there was one thing lacking. I was afraid of women, especially the young ones, slender and fair, whose eyes sparkled above their veils. So I grew to be a man knowing no female save my mother and her servants. My family began to despair of me, for it seemed I would never get married.

One fateful day, as I walked along a narrow street in the city, a gang of giggling, chattering girls came towards me. Alarmed, I shrank back into a corner until they had passed. But at that moment, across the street, an upstairs window opened and a girl appeared, who began to water flowers on the window-sill.

She was so lovely that her face would have made the moon hide itself in the clouds from envy. At once I forgot my fear of women and I fell madly in love. She saw me staring at her open-mouthed. With a mocking laugh she closed the shutters, leaving me filled with a new feeling of terrible desire.

While I stood there rooted to the spot, the alley was filled with noise. A richly dressed man, riding on a mule and surrounded by slaves, stopped at the door of that very house.

Dismounting, he went inside, followed by his attendants. My heart sank, for he was none other than the kadi, or chief judge, and I knew he must be the father of that vision of loveliness. Now I could never hope even to meet her, let alone win her love.

Sick at heart, I went home and crawled into bed. I could not, would not eat, so dark was my despair. Day by day I grew weaker. Doctors were called. Medicine did not help. My family were at their wits' end.

Then an old servant looked at me and said, "I know what is wrong with you, sir. Tell me the name of this girl who has stolen your heart." When I told her, her eyebrows rose into her white hair. "Oh, oh, you aim high. Still, let me see what I can do."

I offered to reward her with gold, but she said, "Results first, rewards afterwards," and left me. Two days later she returned. Her face was sad. "Alas, my boy," she said, "pretending to be a holy woman, I got to see the kadi's daughter. But she laughed and told me to be gone."

My misery knew no bounds. I turned my face to the wall and prepared to die, despite the pleas of my family. But in another two days the old dame came back, smiling all over her wrinkled face:

"Rejoice, my son. When I told the kadi's daughter you were dying of love, her heart softened. She will see you."

I leapt up despite my weakness, and began to dress. Then I stopped. "But what about her father?" The old dame cackled. "Ha, if a woman wishes to do something, no man can prevent her. Now listen: on Friday morning, the kadi will go to the mosque for prayers. Go to the house, climb the outside stairs which lead directly to his daughter's apartment, and for an hour you will be alone together."

From misery to ecstasy in one moment!

My appetite came back. My family were overjoyed, though neither I nor the old woman told them what had cured me. The only illness I had now was a fever of impatience. I bought new clothes and prepared a costly present for the kadi's daughter.

Everything was in order when Friday morning came. There was just an hour to go before my rendezvous.

Then I made a fatal mistake. I decided I must be shaved, and sent my servant for a barber – a discreet barber, since I wanted a shave, not a conversation.

Alas for my folly and my innocence!

In came an old man, tall and imposing, dark-faced, white-haired, long-nosed, sharp-eyed. He greeted me ceremoniously: *"Salaam Aleikum!"*

"Aleikum Salaam!" I replied, and waited for him to begin, for time was slipping away. But instead of shaving me, the barber offered to bleed me after my illness. My father, said he pompously, often had this done.

I shook my head, not wanting a debate. He said, "Well, perhaps Friday is not the right day for blood-letting. But let us first see whether this is an auspicious day or not."

He opened his bag, took out basin, razor, scissors, brushes, pomade, rose water. But all these he put to one side. "Aha," said he, and held up an astrolabe. To my astonishment he marched into the courtyard and began to make observations of the heavenly bodies.

"Come back and shave me," I commanded.

He took no notice, but continued his astrological studies for several minutes. Then he came back into my room with a grave face. "Not an auspicious day at all," he declared.

"Never mind," I told him crossly, for a quarter of the hour had already gone by. "I do not wish to be bled."

"Ah," said he with a severe look. "It is not blood-letting we are thinking of. I fear that today is not auspicious for an enterprise you have in mind – about which I will not enquire. Discretion is my strongest point, next to silence. There is nothing worse," he rambled on, "than those bristle scrapers who cannot shave for talking all the low gossip of the town."

"Barber!" I cried, my exasperation getting the better of me.

"Barber, indeed," he replied, "but more than that: I am a scientist, philosopher, expert in religion and folklore, with an unrivalled knowledge of the world."

I gritted my teeth. "Shave me or leave this house!"

"Your father," he answered sadly, "if he were alive today (may his soul rest in peace) would never have let his temper get the better of him." Then, looking shrewdly at my red and furious face, he began to soap his brush and get to work.

"A man of my calling must ever be discreet. Do you know what they call me in this city?"

I thought of a number of names, but choked them back.

"I am called El Samit, the Silent One."

"You astonish me," I answered sarcastically.

"But indeed," went on the barber calmly, "my brothers, on the other hand (and God has granted me six) are renowned for their lack of good sense and for talking too much, as I could relate to you, if you wish."

I leapt up, throwing aside the towel. "Your brothers can go to the…"

He stared at me. "Have I by mischance offended you?" He thought for a moment. "Aha – now I realise why you are so upset. You are impatient to leave for a rendezvous and, if my instincts are correct, with a woman. And, since the hour of prayer is at hand…"

"I know, I know!" I shrieked.

He went on, "This can only mean that her father, or even her husband, will be absent. No wonder the heavens warned against your enterprise!"

This was too much. I wiped the soap away with the towel, threw on my robe and turban, gave the barber a gold piece and rushed from the house, while he called after me, "At least let me come with you, to be sure you return home safely."

His voice rang in my ears as I fled through the back streets. But alas, the scoundrel followed me at a distance. Out of breath, I reached the kadi's house and crept up the outside stairs. The door opened to my impatient knock. My love looked more beautiful than ever.

"Why have you waited so long?" she smiled. Shamefaced, I began to explain about the fiendish barber, but she only laughed, "I mean, why have I never met you before? Come, let us waste no more time."

And no more we did. But hardly had we sat down, when the street outside rang with the shouts of men and the clip-clop of hooves. The kadi was coming home. My love looked at me. "Why so anxious? My father never comes to my apartment unannounced."

My fears vanished. But suddenly from downstairs came the sound of beating and a terrible howling. The kadi was punishing one of his slaves. And we were not the only ones to hear. Outside in the crowded street, the confounded barber heard the slave's cries and bellowed, "They are killing my master in there. Save him, good people!" And with that, he began to pound on the street door.

The kadi himself opened it and the shameless scoundrel said accusingly, "You are beating my master. Release him."

The kadi was bewildered. "What is your master doing in my house?'"

"Father of lies, you know very well," cried the barber. "He is upstairs with his sweetheart, your daughter."

Astounded, the kadi could only say, "Good people, go up and see for yourselves. There is no such man in my daughter's room."

As the crowd tramped up the stairs, my love did not even blink. "Quick," she whispered, "hide in this trunk. No one will see you. Later on you can come out and…"

Alas, she reckoned without this master of all iniquities, this barber. He rushed in, cast a quick glance round the room and spotted the trunk. Then he and one of the crowd hoisted it on their shoulders and carried it downstairs, with me inside. But halfway down they stumbled. The trunk flew into the air and crashed down in the street. Bruised and battered, I rolled out and in the noise and confusion hobbled away. But alas, my leg was broken.

Yet even then, that fiend continued to follow me, offering his "advice". I crawled home, took a large sum of money and that night left Baghdad for ever. I thought that here, in this distant city, I would be safe, but behold, the cursed barber has followed me here.'"

When the sultan heard the story of the lame young man, he said immediately, "Let this barber be found and brought to me. I shall hear his story."

This was done. The barber, ancient, white-haired and sharp-eyed, appeared before the sultan. Charged with all the harm he had done, he answered boldly, "It was ever thus, O Lord of Time. Let a man seek to do good and his name will be blackened."

"What of the young man's broken leg?"

"Broken leg?" cried the barber. "If I had not saved him, he would have lost his head."

At which forthright answer, the crowd in the city square roared with laughter.

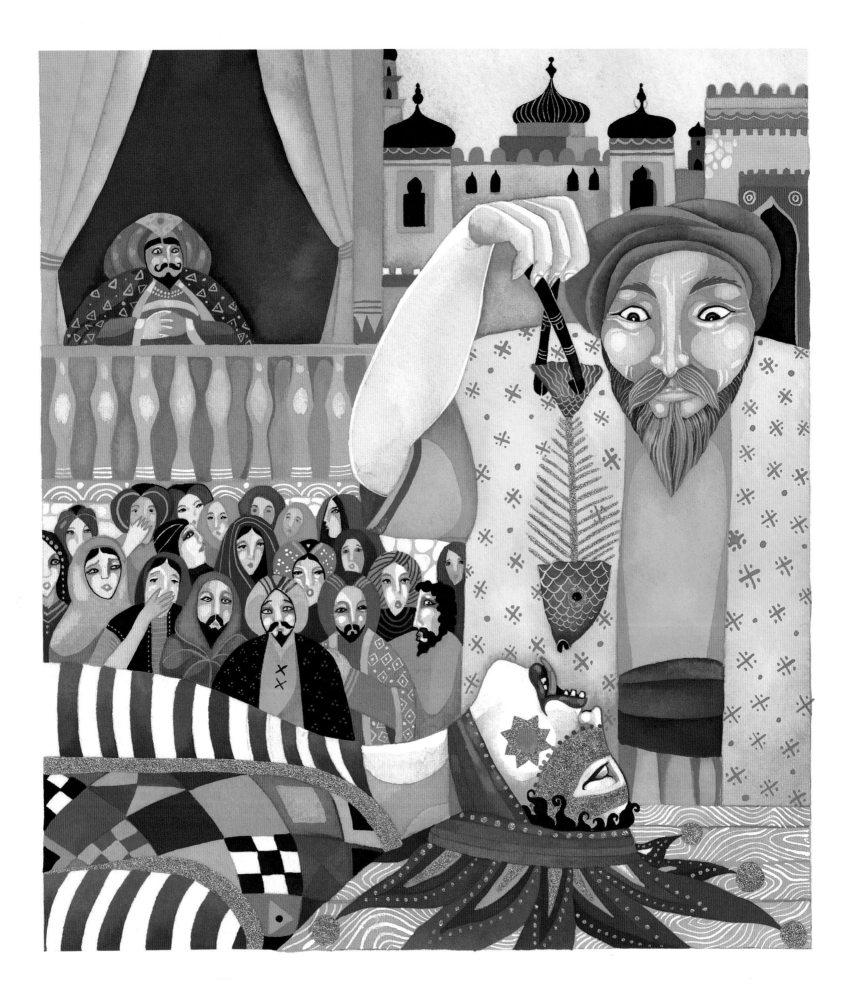

The sultan raised his hand for silence and spoke:

"Truly you are an ingenious barber. But let us see if you can succeed where these four have failed. Tell me a tale which will save their lives."

"Majesty," answered the barber, "nothing would be easier for me. The adventures of my six brothers alone would keep you rooted to the spot for a whole day. But first may I ask why these men, clearly all honourable citizens, must die?"

When the whole account of the many deaths of the jester had been given to him, the barber asked, "May I be permitted to see the dead man?"

"There he lies."

The barber bent for a moment and looked keenly into the face of the unfortunate little jester. Then he rose and declared, "Sire, there is no need for these four to die."

"How so?" asked the sultan, greatly astonished.

"Because, O Prince of your People, the jester is not dead."

So saying, the barber took out a jar of ointment and a pair of pincers. Rubbing the jaws of the jester to soften them, he forced open the mouth, plunged in his pliers, then held a large fishbone aloft to the silent crowd.

Suddenly the jester blinked, gasped, wriggled and then leapt to his feet.

"What a splendid audience!" he cried. "Now, if I may be permitted, I shall tell a highly amusing joke, after which I shall make a small collection."

The multitude rocked with laughter, and the sultan joined in. He called up the executioner and paid him for his services. Next, he rewarded the barber and compensated the tailor, the physician, the steward and the broker for their ordeals and sent them on their way.

"And what shall be my reward, O Master, for all I have suffered?" demanded the jester.

"Your reward," retorted the sultan, "is to be spared the beating you richly deserve for staying out all night."

Once more, the whole square resounded with merry laughter and then the crowd dispersed, each one to work or to home.

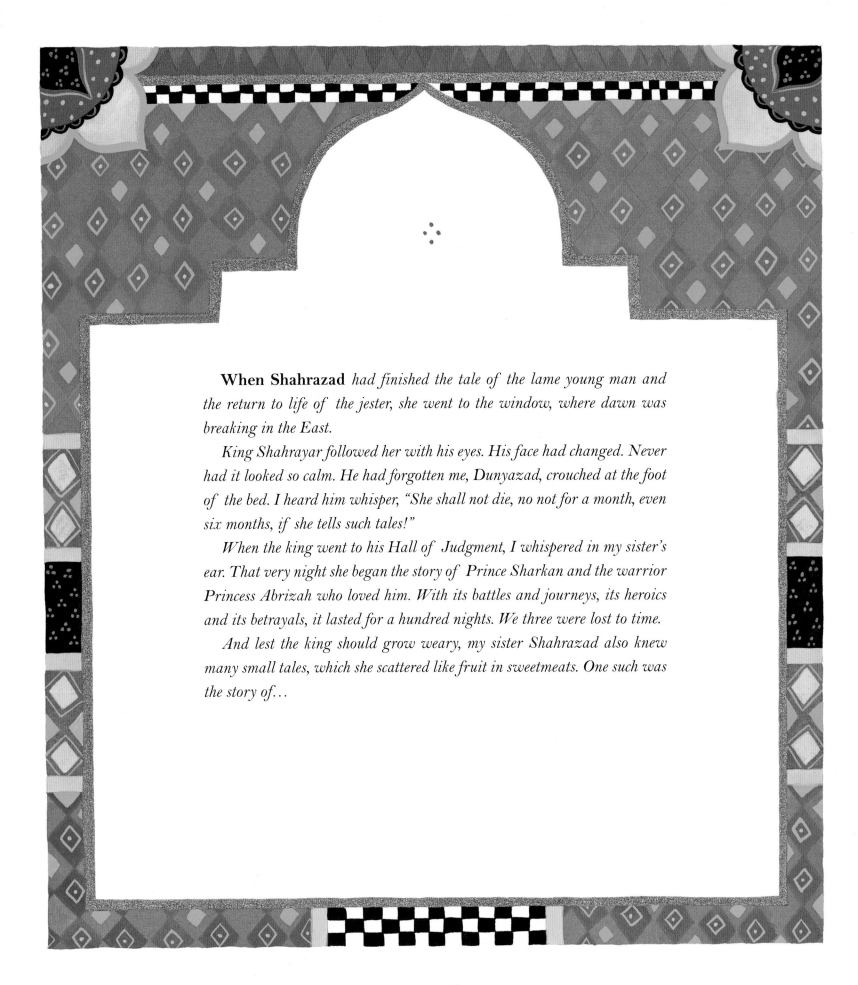

When Shahrazad *had finished the tale of the lame young man and the return to life of the jester, she went to the window, where dawn was breaking in the East.*

King Shahrayar followed her with his eyes. His face had changed. Never had it looked so calm. He had forgotten me, Dunyazad, crouched at the foot of the bed. I heard him whisper, "She shall not die, no not for a month, even six months, if she tells such tales!"

When the king went to his Hall of Judgment, I whispered in my sister's ear. That very night she began the story of Prince Sharkan and the warrior Princess Abrizah who loved him. With its battles and journeys, its heroics and its betrayals, it lasted for a hundred nights. We three were lost to time.

And lest the king should grow weary, my sister Shahrazad also knew many small tales, which she scattered like fruit in sweetmeats. One such was the story of…

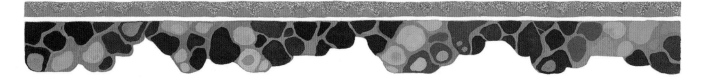

The Dream

It is related, O Happy King, though only One on High knows all that is hidden in the past, that once in Baghdad lived a merchant who was wealthy but not wise. He flung his gold to the wind like rain and soon enough he was as poor as a road-sweeper.

Earning his daily bread and little else, he lay down exhausted each night and slept until dawn. But one night he had a strange dream. A man told him: "Go to Cairo. Your fortune lies there."

"Why not?" thought the merchant, when he awoke. "What keeps me here?" So he set out on foot, and after many a weary month of travel reached the outskirts of the great city by the Nile. He had no money left to pay for lodgings, so he found a corner in the courtyard of a mosque and slept on the bare ground.

As ill luck would have it, that very night thieves broke into the mosque. The police were soon on the spot. They missed the burglars but caught the Baghdad man, half asleep, beat him and threw him into jail.

After three days the wali came to question him, and soon realised this was no Cairo villain.

"Where are you from, stranger?" he asked.

"Baghdad, sir."

"Then why come here?"

The merchant replied, "A dream told me fortune awaited me in Cairo."

The police chief began to shake with laughter, and said, "Dreams are for fools, my friend. Why, only the other night, I myself had a dream about Baghdad."

"Baghdad, sir?"

"Indeed," went on the police chief. "I dreamt I was in a ruined house, at the end of a paved, tree-lined street. The garden had a broken-down fountain in it with a small statue of a lion. I saw it clearly. A voice told me 'Dig beneath the fountain. There you will find treasure.' But before I could dig, I awoke."

The man from Baghdad listened in silent amazement. The police chief held out a handful of coins and said, "Go home, my friend. Seek a better life where you belong."

The merchant wasted no time. He thanked the police chief and returned to Baghdad, this time with a light heart and step. For he knew that the ruined house described in the dream was his own.

Once home, weary though he was, he went straight to the ruined fountain in the garden and dug. Sure enough, in the soil lay a great treasure, enough to bring him happiness for the rest of his days!

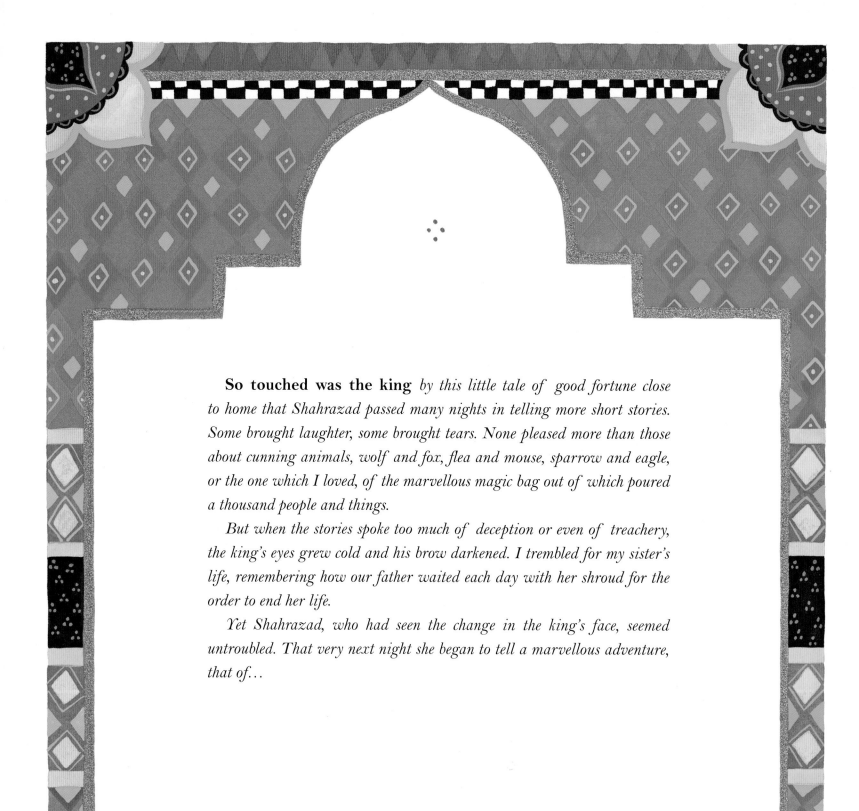

So touched was the king *by this little tale of good fortune close to home that Shahrazad passed many nights in telling more short stories. Some brought laughter, some brought tears. None pleased more than those about cunning animals, wolf and fox, flea and mouse, sparrow and eagle, or the one which I loved, of the marvellous magic bag out of which poured a thousand people and things.*

But when the stories spoke too much of deception or even of treachery, the king's eyes grew cold and his brow darkened. I trembled for my sister's life, remembering how our father waited each day with her shroud for the order to end her life.

Yet Shahrazad, who had seen the change in the king's face, seemed untroubled. That very next night she began to tell a marvellous adventure, that of…

The Ebony Horse

It has come to me, O Auspicious King, that once in ages past there lived a king of Persia who loved the arts and sciences. Nothing pleased him more than to celebrate Nan Roz, the spring festival, by rewarding great inventors or magicians.

There came to him three such men, one from India, one from Greece and one from Persia. The Hindu sage presented the king with a statue of a warrior made of gold and holding a trumpet. One blast from its horn, said he, would paralyse an enemy with fear.

"Truly a wonder," declared the king.

The Greek inventor brought forward a jewelled peacock surrounded by four and twenty chicks. The peacock marked each hour that passed by flapping its wings and pecking a chick. Every month it opened its beak to display a crescent moon.

Marvelling, the king beckoned to the Persian, whose slaves hauled into the throne-room a horse carved of black ebony, a thing of power and beauty.

"Tell me, O wise one," asked the king, "of what use is this statue?"

"Behold, Majesty," replied the magician. He mounted the horse, touched its neck and, to the bewilderment of the assembled courtiers, the magnificent wooden steed soared into the air, until it was no bigger than a bird. While the king and nobles marvelled, the ebony horse flew down from the skies and landed again before the throne.

Clapping his hands, the king cried, "All these inventions are miraculous. Name your desires and you shall have what you will." Without hesitation, the three sages bowed low and said, "Sire, you have three daughters. Let us marry them and remain in your service."

The king consented, and at once the court began to prepare for the celebration – all save one. The king's youngest daughter, watching through the throne-room lattice, saw that her allotted husband, the Persian, though wily and wise, was as old as the hills and as ugly as sin. The princess became so distressed at the thought of being tied to this ancient man that her brother, the Prince Kamar al Akmar, who loved her dearly, went to the king and pleaded with him, "My Lord, do not force our sister to wed

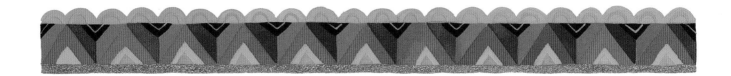

this ghastly creature."

The Persian magician, however, had overheard the prince's words. Masking his fury, he stepped forward and urged the king, "Let His Highness try the ebony horse for himself. He will see that my gift is indeed worthy of the gift of his sister."

Kamar al Akmar had the spirit of adventure in him. Without thinking, he agreed, and sprang into the saddle of the flying horse.

"Turn the knob next to the right ear, Highness," the wily magician told him.

The prince did so, and in an instant the black horse trembled into life and launched itself upon the air. Soon it had vanished from sight, while the king and court applauded. Then they awaited the sight of their prince returning. But after an hour had passed with no sign of Kamar al Akmar, the king demanded of the magician, "What has happened?"

"I fear," said the cunning sage, "that His Highness left so hastily, I was not able to tell him how to control the horse."

In his heart, though, the magician was full of glee at his revenge for the insult he felt he had received from the prince. His pleasure lasted but a short while. He was flogged and flung into prison, while the court went into deep mourning for Prince Kamar al Akmar, who, it seemed, was lost for ever.

Meanwhile, the prince on the flying horse rose higher and higher until the sun threatened to burn him to a cinder. But he was no coward and no fool. Understanding the trick the magician had played on him, he searched the head, neck and back of the horse until he found another knob behind the left ear. This he twirled, and at once his mount began to sink towards the ground.

As the day drew to its close, the prince saw that he was floating above a country far from his own. Below him lay the walls and towers of a fabulous city – San'aa.

He landed, not on the ground, but on the roof terraces of a palace so splendid, it could only be that of a king. Dismounting and drawing his scimitar, the prince explored the great building, passing on tiptoe down stairs and along passages. Suddenly through an archway he saw a richly-furnished bedchamber.

Stepping silently over the sleeping guards who lay by the door, he entered the room, and for a moment his heart ceased to beat. Lying on a couch with her long hair about her shoulders was the most beautiful princess he had ever seen.

Without thinking, he sheathed his sword, knelt down by the bed and kissed her gently. Her eyes opened. She spoke in wonder. "Who are you? I thought I was dreaming."

"I am your slave and, if you allow me, I will be your love," he answered.

Around them the slaves awoke. Girls screamed. Men rushed in, blades drawn. But when Kamar al Akmar faced them boldly, they changed their minds about attacking him and instead ran to the king.

In an instant the king was at the scene, sword drawn and crying, "Who dares invade the palace of the King of San'aa and his daughter's room? He shall die."

But Kamar al Akmar met him blade for blade, calling out, "I am Prince Kamar al Akmar, son of the king of Persia. By chance I am come here. By choice I would remain, for love of your daughter."

The king was impressed by these passionate words, and answered, "How do you expect to win her, alone as you are, brave as you may be?"

Looking out at the pale dawn sky, the prince said, "When daylight comes, O King, draw up your army on the parade ground. I will face your warriors one by one or all together, to win your daughter."

This was done. Hardly had the sun risen, when Prince Kamar al Akmar faced the ranks of the mighty army of San'aa. At a distance the soldiers admired his handsome features and his bravery, but thought him mad. When the prince asked the king, "Have my horse brought down from your roof," they were sure he had lost his wits, and pitied him.

But as the ebony horse was hauled down into the square and the prince mounted, the laughter died in their throats. For no sooner had the prince leapt on its back, than the black steed soared up like a bird into the sky, leaving them and the palace far below.

The prince flew back to Persia to find the whole capital city in mourning.

But this quickly turned to rejoicing when he landed. The king ordered a great feast and in his joy he even freed the Persian magician. Celebrations went on for many days.

Yet the prince's mind and heart were still in far distant San'aa. One night, he stole from the feast, went to the place where the ebony horse was kept and swiftly flew south. Before dawn was grey in the east, he had landed again on the palace roof and was creeping to the room where he knew his love would be lying.

But sleeping, no. She lay awake telling her servants how she missed the lover she had found and lost in a single night. Picture her joy when, finger on lips, Prince Kamar al Akmar appeared at her bedside! Taking her in his arms, he promised that he would come to her again and yet again, until her father consented to their marriage.

She whispered, "No. Take me with you now."

So passionate and forceful were her words that the prince hesitated no longer. He led her to the ebony horse, helped her to mount behind him and, with arms around his waist, sent the flier soaring to the heavens, then northwards towards Persia.

This time he did not land in his father's palace, but in a garden outside. Bidding the princess wait for him, he went and asked his father to come with a splendid escort of soldiers and slaves to bring home his bride-to-be.

He was gone no more than an hour. But imagine his horror and distress when he and the king and his nobles came to the garden to find that the princess and the ebony horse had vanished! It was soon clear to all what had happened. The wicked magician, now free and still tormented with desire for revenge, had found his way to the garden, tricked the princess into believing he was the prince's messenger, and carried her away on the flying horse.

Not daring to land anywhere in Persia, the cunning sorcerer took his captive to another country, where he landed the horse in a meadow outside the capital city. But there lay his mistake; for the king of that country, out hunting, discovered the pair. His slaves seized them and before night had fallen, the princess was lodged in the king's harem and the Persian found himself once more in jail. The horse, marvelled at but not understood, was placed in a storehouse.

The king planned to have the princess for himself, but she refused his offer. Partly from despair, partly to protect herself, she appeared to go mad, refusing to eat and uttering doleful cries.

Meanwhile, Prince Kamar al Akmar, on foot and disguised as a merchant, wandered from city to city, enquiring of people he met if they had seen a fair maiden, a foul old necromancer and a horse made of black ebony. He was treated kindly, for all believed him mad. But none could help him.

Months passed. The prince's feet grew sore and weary, but his courage and the memory of his bright love carried him on, over plain and mountain, forest and sea, until at last, late one night, he came to a city. The guards, suspicious of this stranger, put him in jail. But the jailer was kinder; he fed him and chatted to him through the night.

While they talked, the prince heard someone cry out in one of the cells. "Ah," said the turnkey, "that's the Persian madman."

"Why is he here?" asked the prince cautiously.

"He came here with a fair princess and a great carved horse. The king put the fool in prison and the girl in his harem. But he's no better off for it, because she, too, is mad. There's a rich reward for the one who can cure her, but she is beyond the care of doctors."

At once great joy seized the prince's troubled mind. In the morning, he persuaded the guards to take him to the king. "Majesty," he said, "Know that I am a physician skilled in treating the insane. I can cure your princess."

"And how will you do that?" asked the king, doubtful and eager at the same time.

"The secret of the lady's dementia is in the horse you have concealed in your storehouse. From this horse comes the influence which plagues her. Place the horse in an open space, bring the princess to me and I will set her on the beast, while my spells subdue the evil spirit."

The horse was brought to the palace square. Then the princess, wild-eyed, her clothes torn, was led from the harem. She did not recognise the prince in his travel-stained clothes. But when he bent and whispered in her ear, "Be calm. Do as I say. I am Kamar al Akmar," she stopped her moaning and was quiet with joyous wonder.

In a moment, both were astride the horse's back, he clasping her round the waist. Then, as the king and his court gasped in total bewilderment, all three rose into the air and vanished from sight.

There was no end to the rejoicing, both in the chief city of Persia, when Prince Kamar al Akmar came home with his bride, and in the far, fine city of San'aa, when letters and rich gifts reached the king from his future son-in-law.

So all lived in contentment until the Great Separator took them one by one. But that was not to be for many, many years.

And what of the ebony horse? I fear that the king of Persia had it destroyed, lest it should carry his loved ones away once more!

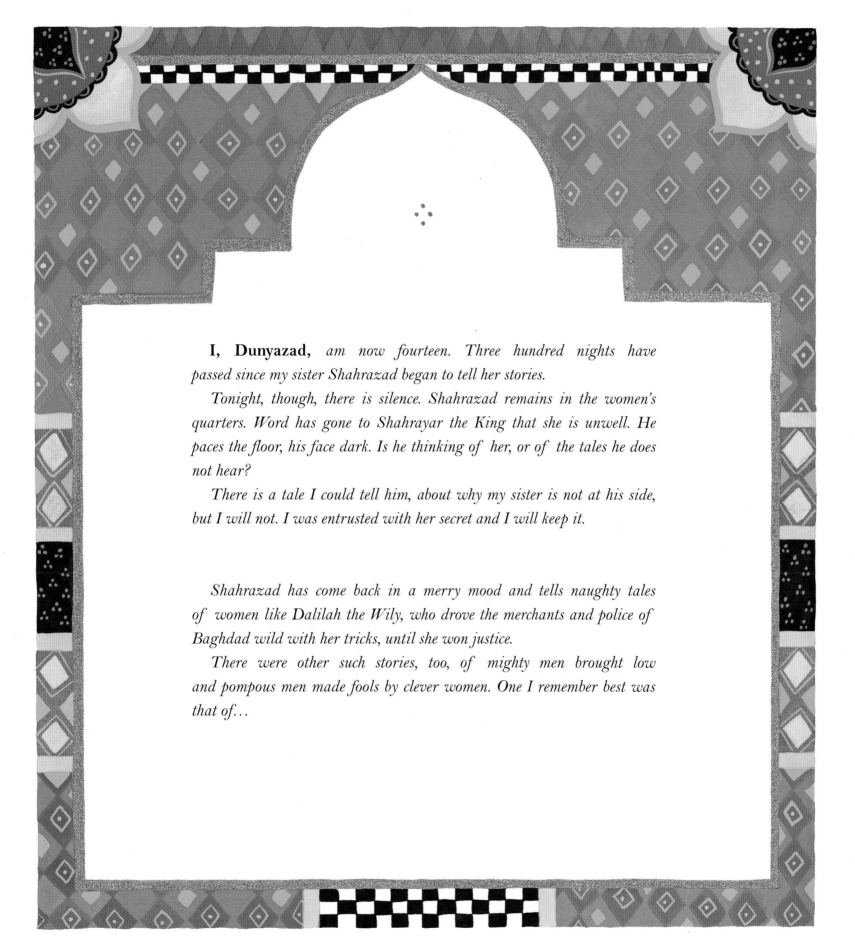

I, Dunyazad, *am now fourteen. Three hundred nights have passed since my sister Shahrazad began to tell her stories.*

Tonight, though, there is silence. Shahrazad remains in the women's quarters. Word has gone to Shahrayar the King that she is unwell. He paces the floor, his face dark. Is he thinking of her, or of the tales he does not hear?

There is a tale I could tell him, about why my sister is not at his side, but I will not. I was entrusted with her secret and I will keep it.

Shahrazad has come back in a merry mood and tells naughty tales of women like Dalilah the Wily, who drove the merchants and police of Baghdad wild with her tricks, until she won justice.

There were other such stories, too, of mighty men brought low and pompous men made fools by clever women. One I remember best was that of…

The Woman with Five Suitors

There was and there was not, O King (for what is certain, save the power of One on High?) in a distant city, a woman both young and fair, admired by men both high and low. Yet she loved only one man, young and handsome.

One day, some jealous person whom the young man had punished in a fight gave false evidence to the police and the young man was put in jail. Yet his sweetheart did not weep. She burned with anger, but only for a while. Then she put her wits to work.

She went to the wali with a humble petition for the release of the young man. When he saw her, the wali licked his lips, but said solemnly, "I will sign his release, but you will have to go to the kadi and get his signature as well."

"How can I thank you?" cried the young woman. The wali smiled. "Nothing could be easier. Just go into the room at the back of my house and I will join you."

She lowered her head. "O sir," she whispered, "it is not right for me to enter your private room. But I would be honoured if instead, you came to my house." And to the wali's glee, she named a time that very evening and went on her way to the kadi.

Stroking his white beard, the kadi said, "Of course, my dear. And you must take your paper back to the wazir, who will countersign it." Then, winking and nodding his head towards the women's part of the house, he went on, "But first…"

"Oh sir," simpered the young woman, "I would be so honoured, but only if you come to my home." And she named a time, ten minutes after her rendezvous with the wali.

Leaving the kadi pulling at his beard in excitement, she went back to the wazir. He in his turn was invited to visit her (ten minutes after the kadi). Rubbing his hands with delight, he sent her on to the king.

"Majesty," she whispered, bending low before the throne. He listened to her plea, then consented to visit her that very evening, when he would sign the paper for her sweetheart's release.

Now the young woman had one more call to make. She went to a skilled carpenter and

asked him to make her a cupboard with four compartments and four doors.

"O second rising of the sun," he replied, "it shall be done. Do not think of paying me with mere money, though. Simply step into my little room behind the shop."

She shook her head. Instead, she bid him join her that evening – a little after her other guests. "And by the way," she said with a smile, "I will have five compartments."

As the sun was setting, the procession to the house of the young woman began. First came the men from the carpenter's workshop, carrying the great chest with five doors. This was set down along the wall of her guest room, where a lavish meal had been laid out.

As the men left the house, the wali arrived, bearing with him the release paper for the young woman's sweetheart. The young woman greeted him warmly. "Why not slip on this hat and gown to put yourself in a party mood?" she said. In no time at all, he was clad all in pink and seated at the table.

But as the first delicious mouthful reached his lips, a great knocking at the outer door filled him with alarm.

"My husband!" cried the young woman. "I thought he was far away."

"What shall I do?" cried the wali.

"Quick – hide in here until he goes away!" she answered, opening the door of the lowest compartment of the chest. He crept inside.

As one door closed on him, another opened to admit the kadi, ready to embrace the young woman. His joy was great, but lasted only a moment. His signature on the release document was still wet as he was hurried into hiding in the cupboard, dressed in festive orange. There he crouched, just above the wali.

After the kadi, it was the turn of the wazir, in bright blue, and last but not least the king, dressed absurdly in brilliant green.

Four guests were now crouched painfully inside the tiny compartments, furious at having been tricked, for each could hear every word spoken outside, but did not dare to utter a word, lest he be discovered.

Now the young woman was about to hasten to the prison with the precious paper to

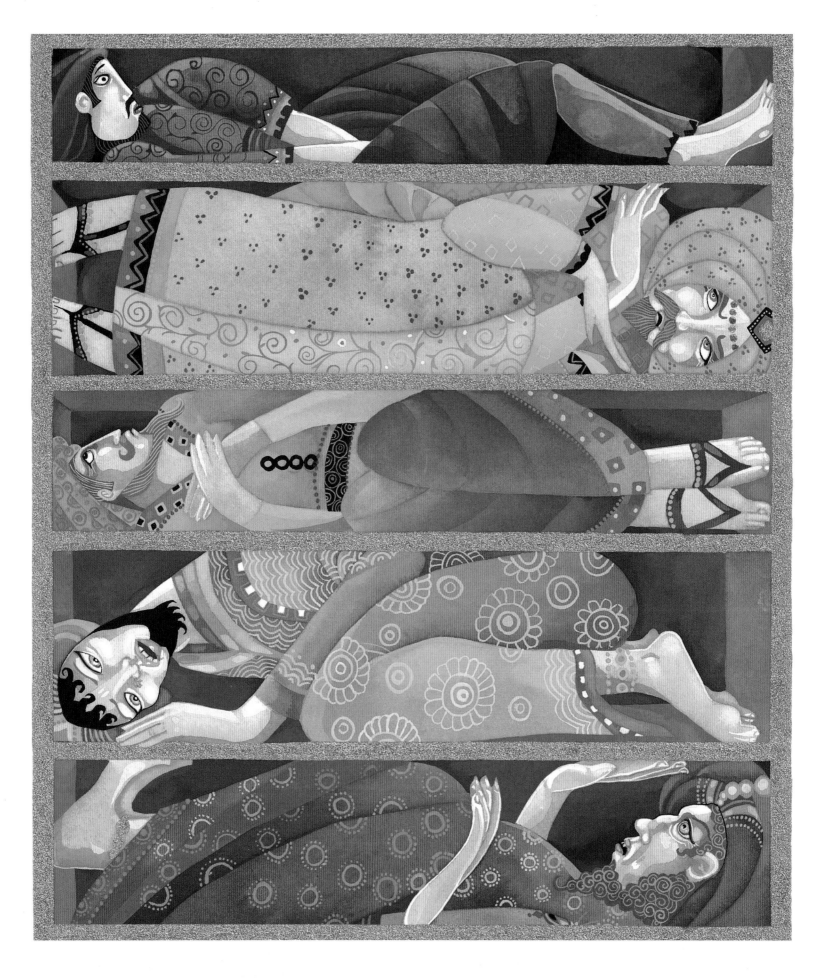

free her lover – when who should arrive but the carpenter, in search of his reward? She greeted him with a rebuke. "You're a fine one. I asked for a big chest. Just look at that top compartment! There's hardly room for anything in there."

"But my angel," cried the astonished carpenter, "there's room up there for a grown man!"

"Ha! Could you get in there?" she demanded.

Without a thought, the carpenter clambered like a monkey into the highest compartment – and in an instant she locked the door on him.

The young woman left the house like a whirlwind, and by dawn's early light she and her lover were far away.

Alas for her suitors! They had to stay where they were. As the hours passed, the king, the wazir, the kadi, the wali and the carpenter, each cooped up in his little cell, began to feel hunger, thirst, and other needs.

Finally the carpenter could bear it no longer. He made water. It fell into the next compartment, on to the head of the king and from him down on to his officers, according to rank.

Lowest of all, the wali cried out in despair, "Is it not enough that I should be stuck like a hen in a coop? Must I be humiliated too?"

"I know that voice!" called the kadi. "We are in the same plight, we two."

"Alas, there are three of us," moaned the wazir. "And my plight is worse. For what if the king should hear of this?"

"He already has," came a doleful voice from the next compartment.

"Majesty," said the carpenter. "We have nothing to lose, all five of us. Let us shout for our lives." And with one voice they called out for help.

At first, the neighbours feared to enter, thinking that evil spirits had invaded the house. But when the wazir shouted, "Ten gold dirhams to the man who sets me free," the doors were flung open and the five bedraggled unfortunates were let out.

Naturally they gave no word of explanation, and each hurried back to where he belonged. It was not long however, before ingenious minds had pieced together the full story of their shame. Yet it was a long, long time before their folly or the young woman's cunning were forgotten.

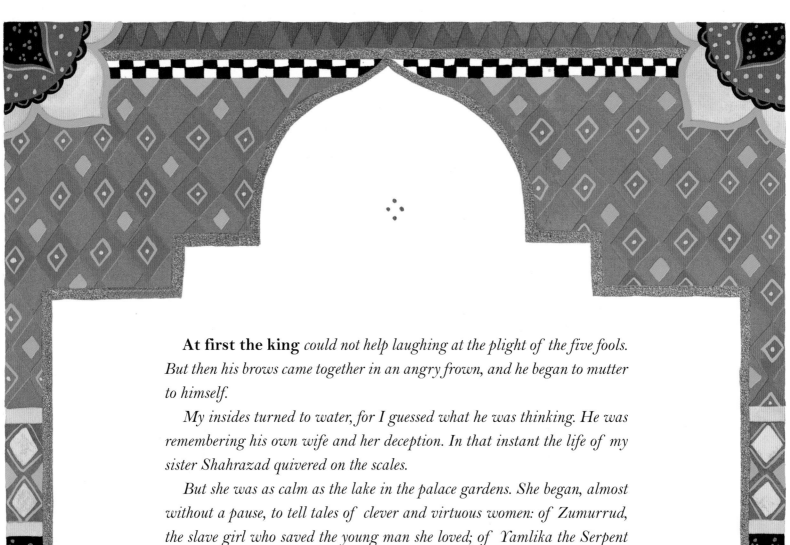

At first the king *could not help laughing at the plight of the five fools. But then his brows came together in an angry frown, and he began to mutter to himself.*

My insides turned to water, for I guessed what he was thinking. He was remembering his own wife and her deception. In that instant the life of my sister Shahrazad quivered on the scales.

But she was as calm as the lake in the palace gardens. She began, almost without a pause, to tell tales of clever and virtuous women: of Zumurrud, the slave girl who saved the young man she loved; of Yamlika the Serpent Queen, beautiful and wise; of Tawadda, who defeated the holy men in a contest of pious learning.

When, after many nights, King Shahrayar was calm again, Shahrazad said,

"There is yet more, O King of Time. Would my Lord like to hear of Marjiana, the quick-witted slave girl, and her fortunate master, Ali Baba?"

The King's eyes gleamed.

"Tell on!" he commanded.

Ali Baba and the Forty Thieves

I have heard tell, O Happy King, that once there lived two brothers. One, Ali Baba, was a woodcutter who married a woodcutter's daughter, and they were poor. The other, Kassim Baba, married a merchant's daughter and had grown rich and proud. As you will see, the two brothers were alike as chalk and cheese.

Each day, Ali went out with his flea-bitten old donkeys to gather wood in the forest. But on this day of all days, he wandered from his usual path and found himself by a sheer rock face. As he pondered which way to turn, he heard in the distance the jingle of harnesses and the sound of men shouting. Who could it be in this desolate spot?

Ali took no chances. Hiding his donkeys in the bushes, he climbed a tree and crouched in its branches. Soon enough, a great band of horsemen, savage, bearded and armed to the teeth, halted before the cliff. Their leader, even bigger and more brutal-looking than the rest, dismounted, and called out, "Open, O Sesame!"

With a grinding roar, the stone split open, revealing a deep, dark cavern. Cursing and laughing, the robbers, for they could be nothing else, unloaded their horses and carried great bags of loot into the cave. Trembling, but still alert, Ali counted them: there were forty thieves in all.

At last, out they came. The leader roared, "Shut, O Sesame!" and with a fearful crash the cliff closed and was as before, with no trace of an opening.

Only when the last hoof-beat had died away did the trembling woodcutter come down out from his hiding-place. Yet curiosity is greater than fear, and he could not resist calling out, "Open, O Sesame!"

Gritting his teeth, he crept into the dark opening. And in the little daylight which came from outside, he saw that this was indeed the storehouse for generations of robbers, with sacks and chests spilling their loads of glittering gold, silver and jewels.

Calling his donkeys to him, Ali Baba took the bags from their backs, emptied out the firewood and loaded them with gold coins until the little beasts could barely walk.

The sun had set when he reached home, and by the light of a lamp he emptied the treasure on to the floor before his wife's astonished eyes.

"Alas," she cried, "has my husband turned thief?"

"No, wife," answered Ali. "I have taken from thieves. Now, help me bury this gold in our garden. No one must know of it, if we value our lives."

"Let us count it, at least," said Ali's wife. But soon, seeing that the coins were too many, she decided to weigh them. "Our scales are too small," she said at last. "I'll go to your brother's wife and borrow hers."

Now Kassim's wife was as mean as her husband, and she was also a busy-body. So when Ali's wife borrowed the large scales, her sister-in-law smeared them with suet. In their haste to weigh and bury the treasure, neither Ali nor his wife noticed that when they returned the scales to Kassim's house, a single gold coin was stuck in the fat.

Imagine Ali's surprise when, next day, his brother appeared at the door, demanding, "How did you get hold of gold like this?" So Ali felt obliged, though his brother had never lifted a finger to help him, to tell him about the hoard. But what was worse, Kassim threatened that unless his brother revealed to him where he had found these riches, he would inform the wali.

Before the morning was out Kassim, gleeful but impatient, was driving a string of ten mules to the forest hiding-place. Using the magic words, he entered the cave and by torchlight greedily began to pile up great heaps of gold and silver near the doorway – which he had closed, so as not to be seen from outside.

Thoughts of wealth, however, had confused Kassim's brain. When he turned to leave the cave, he could not remember the password! "Open, Wheat," he cried. "Open, Barley." "Open, Rye." Indeed, he tried the name of every growing thing except the right one. His torch went out, and he grovelled in terror in the darkness amid the gold and silver.

But not for long. That very day the forty thieves returned to their store. Immediately they were on guard, seeing the mules loose in the bushes. At the captain's command, the cliff yawned open. The luckless Kassim tried to flee, but was struck down without mercy and cut into four pieces. Wiping their swords, the band departed, leaving the gruesome

remains to warn anyone else who might dare to tamper with their treasure-store.

Late that night, Kassim's wife came in tears to her brother-in-law. "My husband has not returned. I fear for his life."

Next day at dawn, despite his own fears, Ali set out for the forest. Soon enough he reached the rock, opened the cavern door and there, on the threshold, discovered the grisly remains of his brother. Mastering his horror, he carefully loaded them on to his donkeys and carried them to Kassim's house.

Kassim's wife fainted away at the sight, and Ali himself was at his wits' end to know what to do. How could they conceal Kassim's death? How could they hide the terrible way he had died?

But, by the will of One Most High, there was in Kassim's household a young woman slave called Marjiana, who was as clever as she was beautiful.

Marjiana knew exactly what to do. First she took gold from Ali and brought an old tailor secretly to the house, blindfolding him so he should not know where he was working. By his skill, Kassim's corpse was sewn together so that no one could tell how he had died. Next, Marjiana went to buy special medicines from the druggist, so as to spread the rumour that Kassim was ill and at death's door.

Soon they were ready to announce his death and prepare his funeral. Once that was safely over, Ali kindly invited Kassim's widow to become his second wife. Not only did he treat her more generously than she deserved, but he placed her son in charge of his father's shop.

So Ali was now a wealthy man and had no more need to cut wood. He had all he and his family could wish for, including the wit and wisdom of his new servant Marjiana.

And soon he had great need of that. For within days the robbers returned to their hideout and discovered that Kassim's body had gone.

"Someone knows our secret," swore the robber chief. "We must find out quickly, and they shall die."

The robbers drew lots, and the chosen one went to town to find out what he could of the death of Kassim. At first he learnt nothing, but after much searching he came across

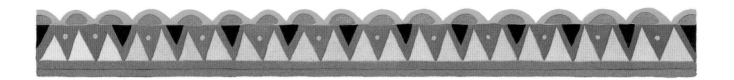

an old tailor who seemed to have more money than he could earn by his trade. With a little more gold in his hand he told the robber the story of the sewn-up body, and by guess-work he led his questioner to the house of Ali Baba. Smiling grimly, the robber marked the gate-post with white chalk and stole silently away.

But wily Marjiana spotted the white cross on the gate. "Someone intends evil against this house," she told herself. Quickly she found a piece of chalk, and soon every house in the street was marked in the same way.

That night, when the robbers crept into the street intent on murder, they found that they had been outwitted. Chewing their lips with rage, they slunk back to the woods. As was their horrible custom, they beheaded the thief who had failed them.

A second one was chosen and he, thinking himself smarter than the first, also bribed the old tailor and, finding his way to Ali's house, marked it with a blood-red cross. But he was no match for Marjiana. Next night the killers found red crosses on every house in the street.

Thus another hapless robber lost his head. The robber chief growled, "This time, I will go myself." He wasted no time in finding the house of Ali Baba, and instead of using chalk or blood, he committed the house to his own memory. Now he was ready for his revenge.

The robber band gathered a herd of mules and placed on the back of each two great oil jars. But only one contained oil. Inside every other jar crouched an armed robber.

The robber chief arrived at sunset outside Ali Baba's gate. Claiming to be an oil merchant who had lost his way, he asked shelter for the night. Generous Ali made him welcome. The mules with their deadly load were left in the courtyard, while the false merchant was given the bedroom overlooking it.

So far, so good, he thought, and he secretly told his men to wait until he gave the sign, by throwing pebbles on to the jar tops. Then they were to creep out in the dead of night and slaughter everyone in the house.

By chance, though, Marjiana found that she needed more oil for the lamps. A fellow-servant laughed and told her, "There are scores of oil jars on the mules outside. Our guest owes us a cupful."

Marjiana went out into the courtyard and one of the robbers, thinking this was his captain coming, whispered, "Is it time yet?" In the twinkling of an eye, Marjiana answered in a low, gruff, voice, "No, not yet. Be still!"

She passed down the line of mules, tapping on each jar in turn and whispering, "Wait!" until she found the last jar, full of oil. But now she had other plans than lighting lamps. With the help of another slave she took the oil indoors and, pouring it into a cauldron, heated it to boiling point.

Then, filling a large jug with the fiery liquid, she returned to the first jar, tore off the top and emptied the steaming oil on the head of the robber inside. He died with a gasp.

To and fro went the resolute girl, until the whole robber band had been boiled to death. And that is how their captain discovered his men when he stole out before dawn, unable to understand why they would not answer his signal.

He wasted no time in mourning, but fled back to the forest hideout. He was alone, his band destroyed. But his thirst for vengeance was now multiplied forty times.

Yet he remained both patient and cunning. He bought himself new clothes and dyed his hair, his beard, even his eyebrows a different colour. Using some of the stolen wealth, he set up business in the town. After some little time he discovered, to his joy, that in the very same market Ali Baba's nephew also had a shop.

The false merchant befriended the unsuspecting young man, inviting him first to coffee, then to sumptuous meals, until Ali's nephew began to feel he must return this lavish hospitality. So he asked his uncle for help and Ali, generous as ever, said, "Invite your friend to take a meal with us this Friday night. He will be welcome indeed."

This was the chance the robber chief had schemed for. On Friday night, he arrived at Ali's house dressed in fine robes and bearing gifts – with a sharp dagger concealed in his clothes.

As his host greeted him, the robber chief said, "I have a request that may seem strange to you. My physician forbids me to eat any food prepared with salt." The hospitable Ali replied, "Think nothing of it," and gave instructions to Marjiana in the kitchen.

But Marjiana was not fooled. She said to herself, "Who is this person, who will

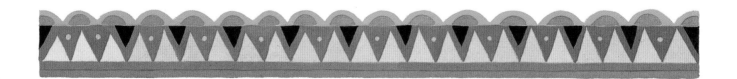

not eat salt with his host? For salt signifies trust and hospitality. I will take a closer look at him."

As she helped the other servants to prepare the table, she observed the guest closely and saw at once that his beard had been dyed. And those fierce eyes were familiar to her. Bending low over the guest to serve him, her quick eye caught the gleam of a dagger. Now she knew for certain who her innocent master was entertaining, and she too made her plans.

Hours later, when the meal was over, Marjiana changed her clothes, let down her long hair and said to Ali Baba, "Is it permitted for your slave to dance before our honoured guest?"

Ali was delighted and, while another servant played the tambourine, Marjiana danced gracefully round the company while they applauded her, none more loudly than the guest.

Now Marjiana drew a dagger from her belt and began a wilder dance. The tambourine boy beat a fiercer rhythm while she brandished the flashing blade above her head swaying from side to side.

Suddenly, to the horror of Ali Baba and his family, the girl threw herself on their guest and stabbed him to the heart. He died quickly and silently, as his men had done.

"What have you done, Marjiana?" cried her master. "You have ruined me. This man was a guest in our house…"

"A guest who would not take salt with you," answered Marjiana, "one with treachery in his heart. This man is none other than the captain of the forty thieves. See this dagger hidden in his robe. It was intended for your heart."

At last Ali Baba saw the truth. "O wise Marjiana," he said, "not once but three times have you saved our family from destruction. I beg you to become one of us."

And so it was. Marjiana became a free woman and consented to marry Ali's nephew. They all lived together in peace and prosperity, for the glittering treasure-store in the forest was theirs to command, now that the forty thieves were no more.

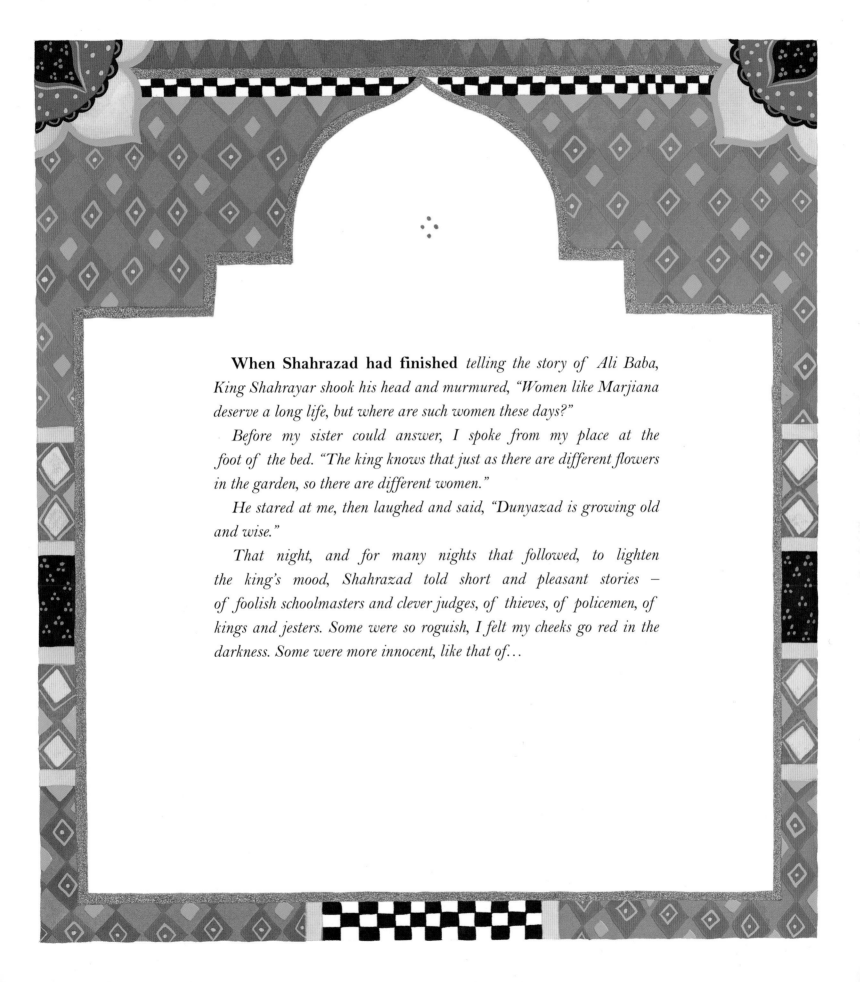

When Shahrazad had finished *telling the story of Ali Baba, King Shahrayar shook his head and murmured, "Women like Marjiana deserve a long life, but where are such women these days?"*

Before my sister could answer, I spoke from my place at the foot of the bed. "The king knows that just as there are different flowers in the garden, so there are different women."

He stared at me, then laughed and said, "Dunyazad is growing old and wise."

That night, and for many nights that followed, to lighten the king's mood, Shahrazad told short and pleasant stories — of foolish schoolmasters and clever judges, of thieves, of policemen, of kings and jesters. Some were so roguish, I felt my cheeks go red in the darkness. Some were more innocent, like that of…

The Donkey

Neither here nor elsewhere, O Fortunate King, there lived a couple of rascals who spent their time making fools of other people – and getting a living from it.

One day they spotted an old farmer on his way to market, leading a donkey on a rope. He seemed deep in thought.

The two scoundrels crept up behind him. Then, while one took the loop of the halter and slipped it round his own neck, the other led the beast quietly away to sell it in the town.

After a while the farmer happened to turn round and saw, instead of his ass, a young man with a sorrowful face at the end of the rope.

"Bless my soul!" he cried. "Where did you spring from, and where is my donkey?"

The thief replied humbly, "Sir, I am your donkey. Because of my sins, and my bad behaviour towards my parents, I was changed into an animal. But today I believe that my ever-forgiving mother has prayed to the Almighty for me – for I have been set free from the ass's skin."

The foolish, kind old farmer took the halter from the rogue's neck, saying, "Heaven be praised for your mother's goodness! But alas, when I think of how often I have beaten you to make you work harder... Forgive me."

The crafty fellow wiped away a tear and said, "There is nothing to forgive. I have learned my lesson. From now on, I will behave well."

"Then may Allah bless you, my son," said the old man as the thief ran away, and he headed for the market to buy himself a new donkey.

Imagine his astonishment when he reached the pens where mules and asses were for sale: there in the middle of them all was his own beast, which the second thief had already sold! Recognising his old owner, the donkey brayed for joy and pushed out his nose, trusting to be taken back.

But the farmer shook his head sadly but sternly. "Oh no, my son," he said. "I see all too clearly that your repentance did not last long and you have gone back to your wicked ways. Well, this time you must suffer for it. Find some other master!"

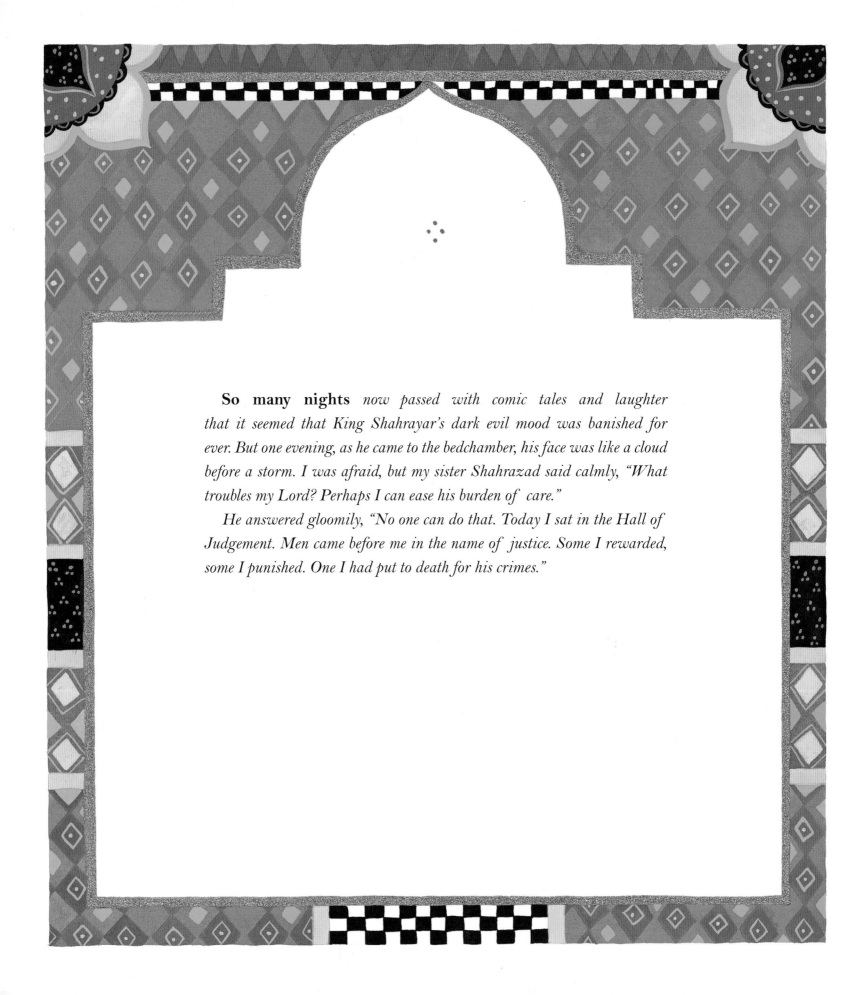

So many nights *now passed with comic tales and laughter that it seemed that King Shahrayar's dark evil mood was banished for ever. But one evening, as he came to the bedchamber, his face was like a cloud before a storm. I was afraid, but my sister Shahrazad said calmly, "What troubles my Lord? Perhaps I can ease his burden of care."*

He answered gloomily, "No one can do that. Today I sat in the Hall of Judgement. Men came before me in the name of justice. Some I rewarded, some I punished. One I had put to death for his crimes."

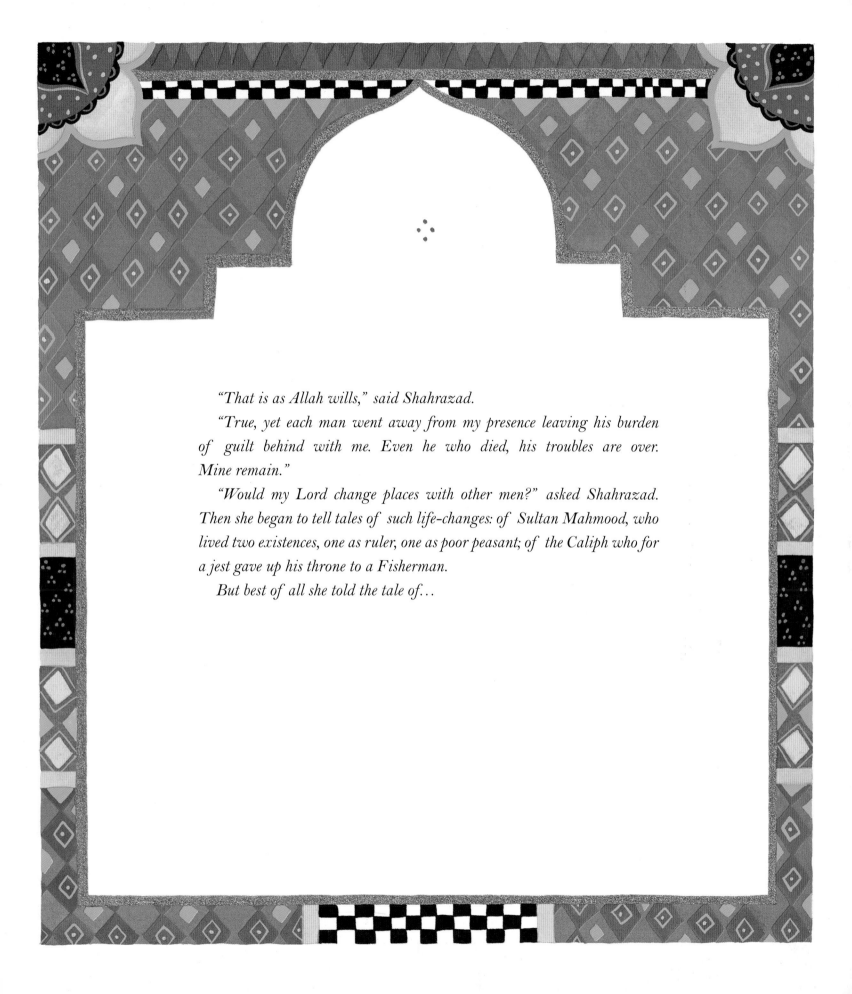

"That is as Allah wills," said Shahrazad.

"True, yet each man went away from my presence leaving his burden of guilt behind with me. Even he who died, his troubles are over. Mine remain."

"Would my Lord change places with other men?" asked Shahrazad. Then she began to tell tales of such life-changes: of Sultan Mahmood, who lived two existences, one as ruler, one as poor peasant; of the Caliph who for a jest gave up his throne to a Fisherman.

But best of all she told the tale of...

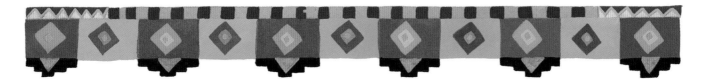

The Sleeper and the Waker

Once upon a time, O King, when Haroun al Raschid, Prince of Believers ruled, there lived in Baghdad a young man named Abu al Hassan. He was fond of life's pleasures and because his father had left him a great fortune, he was able to enjoy himself to the full. Yet he knew that fools and their money may soon say farewell.

So he divided his wealth into two parts. One part he used to further his business as a merchant; the other he spent freely entertaining his friends with food, wine, song and dance. All too soon the money was gone.

So Abu al Hassan went to those who had feasted at his expense and asked them for help. One and all, they turned their backs and refused to know him. At first he felt bitter towards them – then he shook them off like dust from his sandals.

Henceforth, he decided, he would live quietly in his own house with his mother, inviting only one guest at a time to share his rich table. And to avoid being let down again, he brought home only strangers whom he met on one of the great bridges of the city.

Now it happened that one evening, as he stood on the bridge watching the crowds pass by, Haroun al Raschid, the Prince of Believers himself came along, followed by his trusted servant, Masroor. Haroun al Raschid, as was his custom, was disguised, on this occasion as a merchant from Mosul.

Both Abu al Hassan and his unknown guest enjoyed each other's company so much that the host told his new friend the whole story of his life. This moved Haroun al Raschid greatly, and he said, "Tell me, friend, do you have a secret wish, which someone with power might grant you?"

At first Abu al Hassan would not answer, but in the end he admitted, "Sometimes I dream that I am the Caliph of Baghdad and sit in his palace, punishing wrongdoers and rewarding the good."

When he heard this, Haroun al Raschid resolved to play a little trick. Proposing a toast, he slipped a drug into his host's wine. Once Abu al Hassan was fast asleep, Masroor

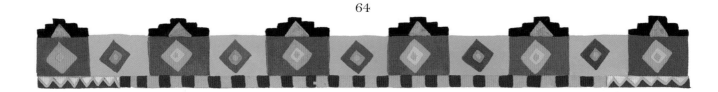

quietly entered and carried him away. Like thieves in the night Haroun and his servant departed. Alas, they left the door of their host's home ajar – and everyone knows that means bad luck.

Next morning the befuddled Abu, his head still spinning from all he had drunk, awoke where he had been placed in the bed of the Caliph of Baghdad. Abu looked around at the fabulous tapestries on the walls, the vivid cushions and rich carpets, and thought, "Where am I? This is surely a dream!"

But then beautiful women slaves entered, bringing bowls for washing and perfumes. "Greetings, O Commander of the Faithful," they trilled. "It is time to rise."

Behind them came a tall slave (that very same Masroor who had carried Abu al Hassan from his own home). Bowing low, he cried, "O Prince, live for ever. It is time for morning prayers and to go to the Hall of Judgement."

"Wait, wait," cried Abu al Hassan. "Are you real or a dream? Tell me – who are you?"

"This humble slave is Masroor, Majesty."

"Then who am I?"

Masroor laughed. "The Prince of Believers is jesting. You are Haroun al Raschid, Caliph of Baghdad."

Abu al Hassan said to himself, "O, fortunate Abu, is this really you?" He beckoned the most beautiful slave to his side. "What is your name?" he asked, and she answered, "Nuzhat al Fuad."

"Then, Nuzhat," he said, "pinch me."

Puzzled, the girl nipped his arm until he squealed with pain. Then he laughed. "I am awake. It is true. I am indeed the Commander of the Faithful."

At that moment, from behind the bed hangings came a strange choking sound. It was Haroun al Raschid himself, hidden there, unable to believe how well his trick had succeeded.

But Abu al Hassan did not hear. He was busy putting on his robes, rich and brilliant. Then he commanded the slaves and soldiers to march before him to the Hall of Judgement.

The real Caliph, now hidden behind the throne, listened in amazement as the pretend Caliph decided all the cases that came before him with wit and wisdom.

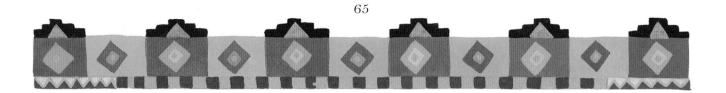

When judgement was done, Abu al Hassan called the Treasurer to him. "Take one thousand gold dinars and go to the house of Abu al Hassan the merchant. Give the money to his mother as a sign of my goodwill towards her."

Next he called Masroor. "Go to the same district of the city, arrest the sheik who governs it, and give him a hundred lashes to punish him for the way he mistreats the poor and insults good citizens."

When that was done, Abu al Hassan went in procession to the banqueting hall, where, watched in secret by Haroun al Raschid, he celebrated in lordly fashion, showing especial favour to the lovely Nuzhat. Alas, his last drink that night was drugged. Early next morning, he awoke in his own bed in his own home.

He gazed around. Where were the ornaments and jewels, the gilded furniture? Where were the servants and soldiers? And where, O where was the gorgeous Nuzhat?

"Ho, Masroor, you idle dog," he called, "come here."

But no Masroor, nor any slave girls came. Instead, his worried old mother hobbled into the room.

"My son, who are you calling," she asked, "and in such a manner? That is not like my Abu."

"Old fool!" shouted Abu. "I am not your son. I am the Commander of the Faithful."

His mother looked round fearfully. "What are you saying? Has my son gone mad? You are Abu al Hassan."

"I am not! I am Haroun al Raschid. I will have you whipped if you do not leave me and send in Masroor," yelled Abu.

Now convinced her son was ill, the old woman stood her ground and pleaded with him. After about an hour's persuasion, his brain cleared and he said, "You must be right, Mother. It was only a dream. Yet it all seemed so real!"

"Yes, yes, my son – a dream. And it was a wicked thing to pretend to be Commander of the Faithful when he has been so good to us."

"How so?" asked her son.

"Why, only yesterday, while you were away from the house, the executioner came

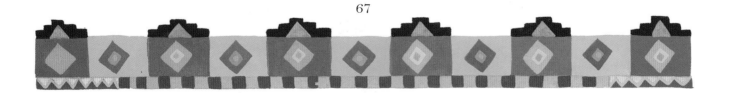

to this district and punished that wicked sheik. And the treasurer brought me one thousand gold dinars."

At these words, Abu al Hassan flew into a rage. Leaping from his bed, he screamed, "Why you old hag, it was I, Haroun al Raschid, who ordered those things. How dare you now tell me I am not Commander of the Faithful? I'll show you!"

With that, he began to beat his mother. Her anguished screams brought the neighbours into the house. Outraged at Abu's violence, they seized him and marched him off to the local madhouse. There he was imprisoned and beaten every day until at last his spirit was broken and he admitted that he was Abu al Hassan. Then he was released.

Many days passed before he felt like going back to his old dining habits. But at last he ventured out to his old waiting post on the bridge. And, as fortune would have it, who should come along but Haroun al Rashid, disguised once more as a Mosul merchant?

At first, Abu al Hassan would have nothing to do with him. But Haroun al Raschid pleaded with him so eloquently that at last Abu agreed to invite him home, and told him of the dream which had turned to nightmare.

"And it all happened because when you went home that night, you left the door open and let in bad luck."

Now Haroun redoubled his efforts to persuade the young man to relax and enjoy the food and wine. Then, at the end of the evening, Haroun decided to try playing the joke again.

Next morning, Abu al Hassan awoke in horror to find himself once more in the glittering royal bedroom, surrounded by beautiful women and powerful men. Even when Masroor prostrated himself before the bed and told him the Hall of Judgement awaited his presence, he was not convinced.

"Son of a thousand dogs," he shouted, "cease this fooling! I am not Haroun al Raschid."

"But, Lord of Time," protested Masroor, "you are indeed he. This is his bedchamber and we are his servants."

Once again, the choking sound came from behind the curtains. But this time it broke into uncontrollable laughter.

"You there, stand forth!" commanded Abu al Hassan.

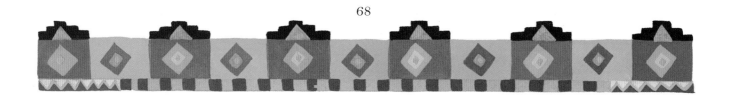

Helpless with laughter, the Caliph emerged from his hiding-place.

"There is the rogue of a Mosul merchant who has caused all my sufferings," said Abu. "Masroor, take him, and give the dog a thousand lashes."

"I cannot," cried the unfortunate Masroor.

"Why not?"

"Because," said Masroor, "He is Haroun al Raschid, Commander of the Faithful."

"Then who am I?" shrieked Abu.

Haroun al Raschid advanced and embraced him. "You are the worthy and much misused man Abu al Hassan."

He explained the whole hidden story of the jest, adding, "Now I and my servants beg your forgiveness."

At this, the whole company bowed low before Abu al Hassan, and at long last he began to laugh. Everyone joined in, until the bedchamber and the whole palace rang with laughter.

Wiping his eyes, the Caliph said, "How may we recompense you for all you have been through?"

Abu hesitated for a moment, then said shyly, "I would like to marry Nuzhat al Fuad, if she will have me."

Blushing with pleasure, Nuzhat came forward and took Abu's hand, while all around them applauded.

Then, loading Abu with presents, Haroun al Raschid sent him home with his new wife, saying as he went, "You are welcome at my palace, friend, whenever you wish."

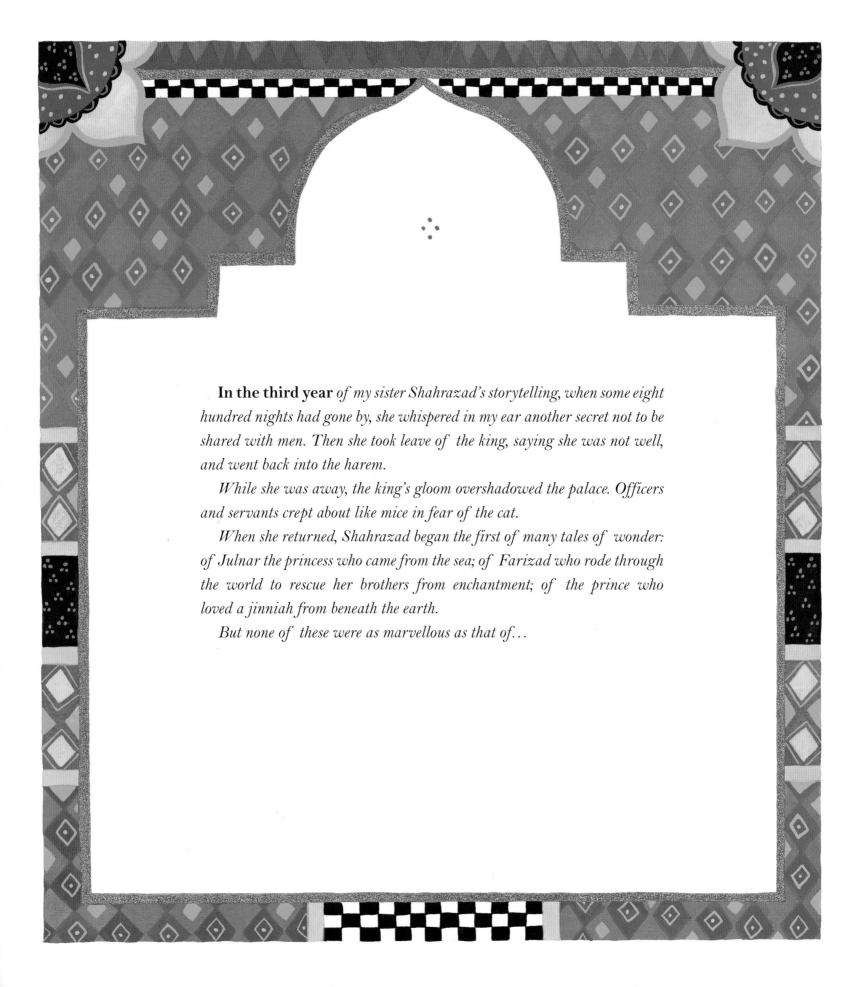

In the third year *of my sister Shahrazad's storytelling, when some eight hundred nights had gone by, she whispered in my ear another secret not to be shared with men. Then she took leave of the king, saying she was not well, and went back into the harem.*

While she was away, the king's gloom overshadowed the palace. Officers and servants crept about like mice in fear of the cat.

When she returned, Shahrazad began the first of many tales of wonder: of Julnar the princess who came from the sea; of Farizad who rode through the world to rescue her brothers from enchantment; of the prince who loved a jinniah from beneath the earth.

But none of these were as marvellous as that of…

Aladdin and his Wonderful Lamp

It is related, though only One on High knows all, that once, in a city in China, lived a poor, honest tailor with his wife, as hard-working as he. They had a son whom they loved dearly, and his name was Aladdin.

He was handsome and quick-witted, but alas, careless and idle. To the sorrow of his parents, instead of working he preferred to run wild in the streets. At last his father died and his mother worked with her spinning-wheel to buy enough food for herself and her son, though he remained as feckless as ever.

One day, as Aladdin played round the market-place with his friends, a man approached him. He was a Moor, tall, richly-dressed but fierce-looking, and Aladdin was afraid. But to his surprise the stranger smiled, and said, "Are you the son of Ali, the tailor?"

"I am," the boy replied, and the Moor embraced him, saying, "Praise be to One Above. I have searched through the world for you. I am your uncle. Tell me, how is my brother Ali, whom I have not seen since we were young?"

"My father is dead," said Aladdin.

"Alas," cried the Moor, "I have come too late… Yet," he added, "it is not too late to pay my family the debts I owe them." And he told Aladdin to go home and let his mother know that he would visit them that very evening.

At first Aladdin's mother was puzzled and suspicious, for she knew nothing of any brother-in-law. But, when the Moor arrived bringing presents and delicious food, her mind eased a little. And when the visitor promised that in honour of his dead brother he would see to Aladdin's upbringing, all her doubts vanished. Surely only a true uncle would care for such an idle, fatherless lad?

Little did they guess that the Moor was a wicked magician!

Next day, the Moor took Aladdin round the market-place and introduced him to the merchants, promising that soon the youth would become one of them. He dressed Aladdin in fine clothes and bought him rich food, until the boy was ready to do anything for him.

However, on the following day Aladdin's benefactor took him, not to the market-places and eating-houses, but out of the city into the barren, hilly country around. Aladdin, unused to walking, began to sulk and grumble, but the Moor sternly urged him on until the boy began to fear this tall, strange, fierce-eyed man.

Soon they came to a desolate rocky place. The Moor ordered Aladdin to gather wood and light a fire. Next, he took from his robe some powder that he threw on the flames. With a sound like thunder and a billowing cloud of smoke, the earth split open to reveal a stone slab with a metal ring set in it.

Terrified out of his wits, Aladdin turned to fly, but the Moor gave him such a blow across the head that he fell down whimpering. In a more kindly manner, the Moor said, "My boy, fortune lies below that stone, which only you can raise. Seize the ring and lift it, saying your father's name as you do so." Trembling, Aladdin obeyed. The stone rose, and beneath it steps could be seen stretching down into a dark cavern.

"Now, nephew, go down through the cavern, making sure you touch nothing until you come to a pillar, on which you will find an old lamp. Bring that back to me and you will be well rewarded."

Seeing the boy was stupefied with fear, the magician placed a ring on his finger. "This will guard you from evil down below. Now go!" and with that, he thrust the trembling Aladdin down the steps into the dark.

Once inside the cave, Aladdin was amazed to see the gloom lit by the sparkle of great chests of gold and jewels. Beyond this treasure-store was an orchard, whose trees were hung with fruit all the colours of the rainbow. Never had he seen such wealth and beauty.

But remembering his orders, he went on until he found the old lamp on the pillar. He pushed it into his robe and turned back towards the entrance. On the way, he could not resist plucking from the trees the red, blue, green and yellow fruit, which he saw were made of pretty coloured glass.

So, loaded down, he came back to the steep entrance and called, "Help me up, Uncle, I beg you." But the Moor was impatient and shouted, "Hand me up the lamp, you little fool. Then I'll pull you up."

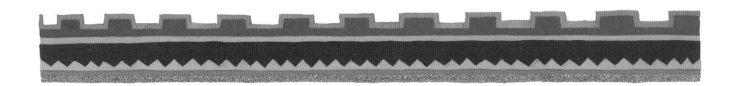

His voice unnerved Aladdin. "Uncle, I am afraid!" he wept.

Aladdin's tears sent the Moor into a rage. He threw more magic powder on to the fire outside, and to Aladdin's horror the earth closed up over him. He was buried alive!

For three whole days and nights Aladdin stayed in the treasure-cave, in a fever of hunger and thirst. Now and then he called out "Uncle!" hoping that the magician would relent and set him free. But the wicked Moor had departed for his own far-off country.

In despair, Aladdin cried out and clasped his hands. And an unbelievable thing happened. Before his eyes appeared a jinni, huge and powerful, with staring eyes.

"What is your will, O Master?"

"Who are you?" quavered Aladdin.

"I am the Slave of the Ring. You summoned me by rubbing it. What is your will?"

"Please get me out of here," begged the boy. And in an instant he was outside again, standing by the ashes of the fire, still holding the old lamp. The jinni had vanished.

Hungry and tired, Aladdin reached home. His mother was shocked to hear of the way the Moor had treated him. Ravenous as a wolf, Aladdin ate everything his mother gave him and slept until the next day, then awoke and asked for more to eat. But his mother shook her head. "Alas, my son, there is not a crust in the house." Aladdin remembered the lamp he had found in the cave. "Perhaps if you sell this in the market it will buy us a meal," he said.

"True, my son. But first I must clean and polish it." And with that, Aladdin's mother began to rub the old lamp with a cloth. At once the little room was filled with the presence of an enormous, ugly jinni, with a voice like thunder.

"I am the Slave of the Lamp. What is your will?"

At first he got no answer, because the poor woman had fainted away. But quick-witted Aladdin cried, "Bring us food to eat – the best."

By the time his mother came round again, the jinni had disappeared, but before her lay a rich feast on gold and silver dishes.

At first she would not eat, fearing enchantment, but Aladdin did not hesitate – he was far too hungry – and in the end she was persuaded to accept their good fortune.

And, indeed, it was good. Every day the jinni brought food on gleaming dishes. And every day Aladdin took the dishes to market and sold them. At first he was swindled, but by and by he met honest merchants. Not only did he get a good price, but he learned much from the buying and selling.

Aladdin made up his mind to work hard and care for his mother. Soon he was doing well as a merchant and had a good reputation. He and his mother lacked nothing with the Slave of the Lamp to hand, though, to spare his mother's nerves, Aladdin summoned the jinni only when he was alone.

One day, Aladdin was busy in the market when he heard the sound of gongs and trumpets and slaves shouting, "Clear the streets. The Princess Badrubadur, daughter of the Great Sultan, goes to bathe. No man's eye shall rest upon her."

Aladdin had not lost his youthful boldness. From a hiding-place he spied on the princess. What he saw nearly made his heart burst. She was so beautiful, she put the risen moon to shame.

At home that evening, Aladdin told his mother that he loved the princess and begged her to go to the Sultan to ask for his daughter's hand in marriage. Despite her fears, his mother agreed to go, such was her love for her son. But she asked him, "How can I go before the Sultan empty-handed?"

"You shall not," laughed Aladdin. Then he showed her the many coloured fruits he had gathered in the cave. He knew now that these were not glass, but precious stones of incalculable value.

Still fearful, but determined, Aladdin's mother carried the jewels in a basket to the Sultan's magnificent audience chamber. Yet her courage failed her and she could not speak. Day after day she returned, and the same thing happened. How many times she might have waited cannot be said, until one day the Sultan noticed her and had her brought to the throne.

When he heard her request, the Sultan was amused, but out of kindness did not show it. Then he saw the basket of jewels – and realised that the young man wishing to marry his daughter was no ordinary subject.

While he was considering what his answer should be, his cunning wazir whispered to him, "Majesty, I remind you that you have promised my son he should marry the princess. At least

delay the decision for three months, to allow me to match this young man's wedding gift."

To Aladdin, three months were three lifetimes. Yet he waited, and the days passed. But on the last day, as his mother was out buying food, she heard the herald in the marketplace proclaiming the wedding of Princess Badrubadur and the wazir's son. The Sultan had forgotten all about Aladdin.

When the royal wedding took place, Aladdin went out of his mind with grief and anger. But he controlled himself and went into his room to summon the Slave of the Lamp.

That very night, the wedding couple, about to get into bed, found themselves lifted by invisible hands and flown through the air. The princess, pale with fright, found herself in a tiny bedroom in a poor house, where a handsome young man, richly dressed, treated her with the greatest courtesy. The bridegroom, however, found himself locked in the privy.

Next day, mysteriously, the couple were back in the bridal chamber. Neither they, nor the Sultan, nor his cunning wazir, could explain what had happened.

On the following night the same thing happened.

And on the third night, though the bedchamber was ringed by armed warriors, the same thing happened once more.

Next morning the wazir's son, his spirit broken by three nights spent shivering in the privy, asked for a divorce. This was granted, and the sultan now turned his mind to the marriage proposal of the unknown young man.

Unwilling to forget his hostility to Aladdin, the wazir whispered in the Sultan's ear, "If this pretender can send you forty gold dishes, borne by forty slaves carrying precious gems, then he will be a fitting son-in-law." He thought this would be impossible for Aladdin to do.

So, too, did Aladdin's unhappy mother. But Aladdin knew better. Next day the city streets were lined with crowds, who watched in awe as a great procession of armed men escorting forty lovely slave maidens bearing jewels, marched to the Sultan's palace. Behind them, shy but proud, walked Aladdin's mother.

When Aladdin, dressed like a prince, came before him, the Sultan was so impressed, he decreed that the wedding should take place immediately. Aladdin, however, asked for a small

delay to prepare a fitting home for his bride.

Thinking Aladdin meant months, the Sultan agreed reluctantly. Imagine his amazement when that very next morning, his servants asked him to come to his bedchamber window. Looking out he saw, at the far end of the city square, a palace whose carved and ornamented roof seemed to touch the skies, while from its doors to the Sultan's home stretched a rich, crimson carpet!

Now, all the wazir could do was to mutter that Aladdin had used evil magic. But his voice was drowned in the sounds of rejoicing as the wedding took place and Aladdin and his lovely bride moved into their splendid mansion.

Years of happiness followed. Aladdin proved a wise prince, generous without limit to the poor, and valorous in leading the Sultan's armies. The Sultan decided that he would leave the running of the country to his son-in-law, which pleased everyone except the wazir.

And one other, who lived in far-off Morocco. Through his spells the magician had discovered that Aladdin, whom he thought dead, was alive and well and about to become Sultan. Mastering his fury, the Moor travelled to China, where he soon saw how magnificently Aladdin lived with his princess. Then, with cool cunning, he hatched a plot.

Buying a dozen new copper lamps, he walked through the city streets calling out, "New lamps for old. New lamps for old." How people laughed! "The man must be mad," they said.

Even Princess Badrubadur sitting with her maidens in the palace could not resist this strange cry from the square below. When one of the servants told her, "Highness, your husband the Prince has an old lamp," she laughed, and told her maid to bring it. So the curious exchange was made, and the mad pedlar departed with the battered old lamp.

No sooner was he alone, than the Moor rubbed the magic lamp and summoned its jinni. Without question the jinni obeyed the evil man's commands – and in that instant, Aladdin's palace was transported thousands of miles to a lonely mountain-top in Morocco.

There the distressed and bewildered Princess Badrubadur was confronted by the Moor. "You will never see Aladdin again," he told her. "From now on, you are mine."

Freezing with disgust, she pushed him away.

"I will come to you again," he said. "We have all the time in the world." Then he laughed, and left her.

Princess Badrubadur was in despair.

Meanwhile Aladdin, returning merrily from a hunt, was surrounded by the Sultan's guards and dragged before his father-in-law. "Where is my daughter? Where is your palace?" the Sultan demanded. Aladdin, stunned by what had happened, could not reply. The wazir whispered in the Sultan's ear, "Now you see that all this was done by evil magic."

The Sultan ordered Aladdin to be beheaded. And his command might have been carried out, but the people of the city armed themselves and stormed the palace, demanding that the life of their beloved prince be spared.

The Sultan reluctantly let Aladdin go, but gave him just forty days and nights to restore the princess.

Distraught with grief, Aladdin wandered weeping through the streets, watched by the pitying crowds. Eventually he found himself sitting alone in a desolate place outside the city. Slowly he realised that his old enemy the Moor had turned the tables on him. Palace and princess must be in Morocco. But how could he reach her? In despair, he clasped his hands – and at once the jinni of the ring stood before him.

"What is your will, O Master?"

"Take me to the Moor's hiding-place!" commanded Aladdin, and before he could blink, the jinni had set him down in the shade of his own palace, under an African sky.

At that very moment, one of the princess's servants opened a window and looked out. Excitedly she called her mistress, saying, "Come and see this man sitting under the palm tree in your garden."

Princess Badrubadur looked out. She saw, in the way only lovers can see, that this was her husband. Quickly she had him brought by a secret stairway to her side. There the pair embraced and wept for joy. Then she told Aladdin all that had happened.

After much thought, Aladdin proposed a plan, to which the princess boldly agreed.

That very night she invited the Moor to her room. She offered him food, sweet wine and even sweeter words. Thinking that she was now his by choice, the Moor ate and

drank greedily down to the last cup, into which the princess had secretly dropped a powerful drug. In a second the Moor's eyes rolled, his knees buckled and he fell to the floor.

At that moment Aladdin sprang from hiding, and with one sweep of his sword, cut off his enemy's hateful head. Plucking the magic lamp from the Moor's robe, he summoned the Slave of the Lamp.

Later that evening, the grieving Sultan looked out of his window, Before his eyes a great shadow seemed to blot out the setting sun. Again he looked, shading his eyes – and behold, the palace of his son-in-law had miraculously reappeared! From its doors, hand in hand, came Prince Aladdin and Princess Badrubadur.

The whole kingdom rejoiced in their safe return, save only the wicked wazir. But he was banished to join his son in a far city, so who cared what he thought?

As years passed, the Sultan died and Aladdin and his princess ruled the realm happily and wisely, until the Great Separator brought their lives to a peaceful close.

Epilogue

A thousand nights and one *had passed when my sister Shahrazad told her last tale. As dawn showed pale in the East, she gave me a sign. I ran to the harem and returned to the royal bedchamber leading a little boy by the hand. Behind me came the nurse, carrying two babies born in the same night.*

Bending low before King Shahrayar I cried, "Pardon my sister, for the sake of her children and yours!"

Now the king wept, and embraced the little ones. "I pardoned her long before I heard their cry," he said. Turning to Shahrazad, he declared, "Allah bless you. I will never harm you."

He summoned our father the wazir, who came with amazement and fear in his face — which vanished like magic when the king spoke.

"Your daughter's like is not to be found. Praise be to Him who appointed her to deliver my people from oppression and slaughter. Your noble daughter has made me repent of slaying so many maidens of the realm."

At once the joyful wedding of King Shahrayar and Shahrazad was proclaimed. But that is not all. The king's brother Shahzaman came from his distant kingdom and asked to marry me. Thus, on one day, two sisters and two brothers were wed, Shahrazad in red and I, Dunyazad, in blue.

Then the king called his scribes to set down for many ages to come, the stories of the Thousand and One Nights.

Glossary of Arabic words

dinar	an ancient Arabian gold coin
dirhan	an ancient Moroccan gold or silver coin
jinni	a mythical Arabian spirit, less important than an angel, with supernatural powers
jinniah	a female spirit with the same powers as a jinni
kadi	the chief magistrate or judge of a town or city
Nan Roz	the Spring festival
wazir	the chief minister
wali	the police chief of a town or city

Sources

The Book of a Thousand Nights and One Night, J. Payne (translation)
(9 volumes, London, 1882-4)

The Book of the Thousand Nights and a Night, Richard Burton (translation)
(16 volumes, London, 1885-8)

The Book of the Thousand Nights and a Night, J.C. Mardrus and E. Powys Mathers
(translation) (4 volumes, London, 1923)

Tales from the Thousand and One Nights, N.J. Dawood (translation) (London, 1973)

The Arabian Nights, Muhsin Mahdi Edition, Husain Haddawy (translation)
(London, 1990)

Glory to Him
whom the shifts of time
waste not away.